Hell in the Zunis

For two years Tobias Cantrell has been a man possessed, searching sunbleached Texas and New Mexico for the Apache who burned his ranch and kidnapped his wife. A determined U.S. Army is driving the Apache into Mexico, but there is no sign of his wife in the wake of destruction.

Meanwhile, Susan Covington has come west in search of her husband, an army lieutenant whose whereabouts are unknown. Fate brings Susan and Tobias together as they search for their loved ones. But someone doesn't want them finding any answers!

The pair must battle killers sent to stop them and uncover a terrible secret the army is keeping – a secret that lies buried within the rugged Zuni Mountains.

Hell in the Zunis

Clay Burnham

A Black Horse Western

ROBERT HALE · LONDON

© Steve Kaye 2006
First published in Great Britain 2006

ISBN-10: 0-7090-7938-9
ISBN-13: 978-0-7090-7938-5

Robert Hale Limited
Clerkenwell House
Clerkenwell Green
London EC1R 0HT

Typeset by Derek Doyle & Associates, Shaw Heath.
Printed and bound in Great Britain by
Antony Rowe Limited, Wiltshire

CHAPTER ONE

A pale gray sky hung low over the sloping hill and swept along its dusty sunburned grass toward a hazy valley. Reining up, Tobias Cantrell glanced only briefly into that valley before dismounting. He loosened the fraying cinches on the secondhand saddle to let his roan blow. He took the buckskin-wrapped canteen from around the saddle horn, gave it a shake and scowled sourly at the empty sound the cap chain made slapping against the small circle of exposed tin. Very slowly he wrapped the canteen's fringed buckskin strap around the saddle horn, then turned toward the valley.

Off in the distance, glazed by dust and haze, sat Fort Craig. Its low structures, built of native stone and thick adobe, were barely visible against the colorless land. There was movement down there in the dust, tiny shadows, indistinct and surreal, like a nest of writhing sand snakes. The blue-bellies would be on the move, herding tired and beaten Indians like cattle in a slow shuffle step toward new lands. Arid deserts fit only for snakes and cactus. Nearly every major fort in New Mexico was hip-deep in Indians, the soldiers disdainful, their commanders bored. The fighting was nearly at an end and there was no more glory to be had. What remained was paper work and hot, dusty marches, a filthy and sweating diaspora of the old and maimed and the very small.

Cantrell's scowl turned darker as he watched the distant swirl of dust. He forced himself not to hope, not even to wish. But it cost him. Extinguishing those better emotions allowed his simmering fury to bubble toward the surface. Desperately he wanted to find Mary down there, but he couldn't allow himself another unanswered prayer.

Despair was already beginning to fill him, every inch. It had been two years. She couldn't be alive, he knew that. Still, he had to know. But the thought of entering another fort, asking the same questions, seeing the same uninterested faces nearly withered his resolve. Then his ire would rise and he'd feel the burning pressure against his face, ready to burst free. She was dead, and nothing he could do would bring her back. But, by damn, he'd know the truth.

Cantrell took a soiled kerchief from his back pocket and wiped his neck and the inside of his stained, tattered hat. He had gotten the hat in Abilene from a road agent who had been no good at his job. Cantrell had taken the rounded-top hat and the few dollars the man carried in his boot, and he took his gun. The road agent hadn't objected. Cantrell had killed him before the man could get off a shot.

It was impossible to tell the time. The sky was a milky gray and uniform as a sheet. The sun didn't penetrate. Cantrell had been on the trail since before sun-up. He had spent many hours in the double-rigged California saddle so he knew evening was coming on. He wouldn't find

6

warm reception at the fort, but he would be able to get fresh supplies.

The roan nickered and tossed its head wearily, bringing Cantrell to full alert. A moment later he heard the thunder of hoofs behind him. Quickly, he mounted and pulled at the reins to head the roan into the oncoming charge. He didn't draw his weapon. That would only make things worse, he thought wryly.

A few seconds later a short column of soldiers crested the hill at a gallop on a line for the fort. At their head was a sharply dressed lieutenant with gleaming buttons and a dark blue hat sporting a shiny double saber insignia of the cavalry centered on the hat's flat point, and a gold acorn band. A gold '9th' pin sat above the sabers.

The lieutenant was young and did not have the experience to hide his surprise at finding a rider in his path. He raised a hand and barked an order. The column slowed to a stop. Riding ahead with the lieutenant was a wiry, hard-faced sergeant. Covered in dust and disheveled, the sergeant kept one hand close by his service revolver.

'Lieutenant Garther, Ninth Cavalry, Company D,' the young lieutenant said, then lifted his chin, awaiting a response.

Cantrell let go a long sigh and introduced himself.

'Where do you hail from, Mr Cantrell?'

'New Mexico.' He knew this was not what Garther wanted to ask, but the lieutenant was following courtesies.

'This is somewhat dangerous country, sir. Do you travel alone?'

'Yes.' He was suddenly quite weary.

'I see. Have you business at the fort, or are you simply passing through?'

'You've got a commander, a Colonel Jesperson. I'd like to see him.'

Garther blinked once then nodded. He had a hard time keeping curiosity from his face but he didn't ask any more questions. 'I would be honored, Mr Cantrell, if you would ride along with me to the fort. I shall be happy to make introductions, if the colonel is about.'

'Thanks.'

Cantrell reined the roan around to face downhill and picked up the trotting pace set by Garther. Behind them, the sergeant bellowed something unintelligible and the rest of the column jumped forward to keep up. Blue or Gray, all sergeants sounded the same. You hardly ever knew what they were saying but you'd damn well better know what they wanted.

Garther said nothing on the ride in and didn't look at his guest. The lieutenant had sized him up accurately as a man who didn't like to talk to strangers. Cantrell found himself liking Garther. He was a man who knew how to treat other men.

Fort Craig sprawled in open fashion on a wide plain of cracked earth and tufts of bunchgrass. The many buildings were aligned along several hard-packed, dusty streets. A central avenue intersected the parade ground where flagpole and cannon stood a lonely unattended vigil. Off to the east about a quarter mile a flat, narrow river wended its lazy way north and south, shaded here and there by stray cottonwoods. The Rio Grande Del Norte.

A pall of dust lay over the camp stirred up by the shuffling feet of a hundred or more Indians. From their clothing and the meager possessions they carried on their backs or dragged behind on travois, Cantrell guessed that these

Indians were from several tribes, not just one. Some wore breechcloths, others wore greasy deerskin leggings. The women wore faded cotton and hide dresses. The colors were as different as the styles.

Most of them were women, with some young children, girls mostly, and some old men. The women were older. No young brides here. There wouldn't be. They would have died defending their homes or children, or their virtue. None of the Indians in the long, ragged line lifted their heads. Their eyes were fastened on the tiny swirls and eddies of dust at their feet. Only a few of the children looked up, staring hotly at the blue-clad soldiers whose boredom had made them blind to the human misery.

There were a dozen mounted soldiers who gently guided the Indians on their slow trek west through the camp toward a corral. It wasn't any more than a cattle-pen, hastily constructed and open to the north wind that brought a bite to the air. The three-pole corral wasn't designed to keep the Indians locked up. It was used more to separate them from the white population. Dirty, deflated, they straggled their way through the rickety gate to sit on the hard ground, no longer caring about their circumstances.

'That's some haul,' Cantrell said flatly. They paused as a squad of foot-soldiers marched past, following the captured Indians.

'Many of them turned themselves in,' Garther said. His voice was tight and he stared straight ahead. 'Not much left of their homes, or anyone left to hunt for food.'

'Where do they come from?'

'Different tribes. Chiricahua, Navaho, Mescalero. Some Mexicans, too.'

9

'No Mimbreños, huh?'

Glancing at Cantrell, Garther shook his head, a sour grin lighting his features. 'No. Thankfully.'

'What'll you do with them?'

'They will be marched to San Carlos, most of them.'

Cantrell shook his head. 'Damn hell-hole,' he muttered.

Curiosity narrowed Garther's eyes. 'You've been there?'

'By and by.' Cantrell turned toward the corral and the pile of human flotsam sitting dejectedly on the cold ground. Spring hadn't yet taken full hold. Evenings and mornings were still frosty. The Indians had little to keep them warm and the soldiers were not handing out blankets. By the time they reached San Carlos half of them would be dead. 'I'd like to talk with them.'

Garther hesitated for a moment, then said, formally, 'That's the colonel's purview. You can bring it up with him.'

Garther pulled up to a hitching-post and Cantrell followed. The small sergeant remained in the saddle and saluted when Garther told him to take the men, see to the horses, and then get supper. Garther watched his men ride off, then wheeled smartly and strode toward a heavy wooden door. Cantrell followed.

They entered a darkened room and for a moment the only thing Cantrell could make out was the pale glow from a pot-bellied oil lamp. A thick, towering black silhouette of a man standing by a large table was caught in the waning light of the day.

Bringing a hand up to shield his eyes against the glare, the man rumbled, 'What do you want?'

Garther closed the door then snapped to attention and

presented a smart salute.

'Lieutenant Garther reporting, Colonel.'

'Oh.' The colonel's shoulders seemed to slump and he turned back to the table where a large, weather-worn oiled-paper map lay, its edges held down with short stacks of books. Slouching over the table, hands flat against the paper, the colonel gazed over the map.

'You have a report?' he asked.

'Yes, sir.'

Feeling anxious, Cantrell moved deeper into the room toward a desk half-hidden in the gloom. On it was another lamp. He scraped a match against a corner of the desk and as it flared to life ignited the second lamp. The room yellowed, catching the pallid colors of the native brick. Cantrell turned the lamp up full until the wick hissed.

The colonel squinted against the light as he wheeled his bulk around to face Cantrell. He looked ready to kill, a giant bear wakened from his slumber. He straightened and his head nearly scraped against the low ceiling. His deep-blue uniform no longer held its crispness, and the yellow piping was faded. He took a deep breath, his face twisting with anger. The movement threatened to burst his uniform seams.

Near the door, Garther hesitated.

'Who the hell are you?'

Cantrell crossed his arms and leaned up against the side of the desk.

'Colonel Jesperson,' Garther said, stepping hurriedly forward, 'may I present Mr Tobias Cantrell, a . . . uh . . . traveler. Mr Cantrell, Colonel Harlow Mayweather Jesperson.' Neither man approached the other.

'Traveler? A damned Reb is what he is,' Jesperson growled.

Cantrell grinned. 'I did have the honor of serving my country in the War of Northern Aggression.'

Jesperson snorted. 'Phah. Get him out of my office, Garther.'

'The war's over, Colonel. For more than twenty years.'

'Then why is it I can still smell the stink of a Reb when I meet one?'

'I'd suggest you see a doctor, but you blue-bellies have the worst sawbones I ever laid eyes on.'

'Garther!'

'I need your help, Colonel.' Cantrell came up off the desk and took a step forward. He marveled at how quickly the old soldier tensed, squaring for a fight.

'We got our hands full.'

'I saw.'

Jesperson let his gaze fall to a small window filmed over with dust and dirt.

'Then you know that with this many Indians under my command I can't take time to help out a saddle bum. Garther, get him a meal, some salt meat. Let him water his horse and fill his canteens. If cook thinks we can spare a little flour, sugar, and coffee, let him have some. Then get him the hell out of my camp.'

Anger flared for an instant in Cantrell. 'I didn't come begging for food, Colonel. I want to talk to you and those Indians out there.'

'The Indians!' Jesperson started visibly and took a quick step toward Cantrell. 'What the hell for?'

Garther sharpened his attention, his own curiosity clearly marked on his weathered but still youthful face.

12

'I'm looking for my wife.'

Jesperson's barrel chest slowly deflated. He started to turn away, stopped, glanced over to Cantrell, then spun about and walked back to his maps. Cantrell glanced up to see Garther look away.

'I gather,' Jesperson said, 'that she didn't leave on her own? Take up with some other man and stick you with an empty house and kids?'

'No.'

Jesperson had absent-mindedly picked up a thick pencil and was tapping it lightly against the maps. Now he tossed it down in disgust.

'Sorry for your troubles, Cantrell. But I can't help you. There've been no white women to come through here for a while. Our trade is in redskins, and it's a damned dirty one at that.'

'No one in your hospital?' Cantrell heard his own voice crack with desperation.

'No one. We've found better than a dozen white women, dead or wishing they were, over the past year. But their men have all identified them. We've got a little girl, maybe ten years old. She spends most of her days screaming. Maybe you'd like to talk to her.'

Cantrell ignored him. 'Some of the Indians you have penned up might know something. I'd like to talk to them.'

Jesperson snorted derisively. 'You happen to take a good look at those people out there? They won't like you any more than they do us.'

'I'm not wearing blue.'

'You don't have to be. You're head to toe in white.'

The disgust Jesperson felt hung thick between them.

13

Here was a soldier, a fighter of Indians. Now he was nurse-maid to them, to beaten, dejected vipers who could strike at any moment despite their docile appearance. His orders, Cantrell imagined, were to get the Indians to their new land and not to waste time or money doing it. But Jesperson was a professional, and more than that, he was clearly human. He knew he was inflicting misery and hated his orders. A warrior doesn't fight old men or women or children. Cantrell had served under such a man many years ago. He had seen the toll war had taken on those who lead.

'Garther says you're taking these people to San Carlos.'

Jesperson stabbed a quick, barbed look at his lieu-tenant. 'What of it?'

'You know as well as I do that half of them in those pens won't make it all the way. A march like that is hell on a fit man. Many of them out there are sick and old.'

Straightening and casting a keen eye over Cantrell, Jesperson said, 'You don't look like a soldier. Of course, never met too many Rebs who understood discipline.'

'I was lucky, Colonel. The years have worn it off of me.'

Jesperson turned away again, his eyes clouded with thought. A small table under the tiny window had a crystal decanter and a stack of glasses. The colonel poured two fingers of a cloudy amber liquid into three glasses. He gave one to Cantrell and another to Garther, dousing the youngster's surprise with a baleful glare. Silently the men toasted and drank.

'A local brew,' Jesperson said sourly. 'But it's all we've got.' He pulled up a chair, sat, took another swallow, and looked up at his visitor, his face open if not particularly friendly.

'You must have been young when you saw service.'

Cantrell nodded. 'Seventeen. Got in fairly early. Had to lie about my age, but I wasn't the youngest. I was seventeen when I killed my first man.'

Jesperson nodded too, filled with his own memories. 'You saw action, then.'

'Served under Colonel Mouton in the Eighteenth Louisiana Infantry. A private. Nothing more than cannon-fodder. I saw a lot of action.'

The Confederate colonel's name caught Jesperson's interest. 'Mouton? You were at Pittsburgh Landing?'

Cantrell took a long slow breath, forcing down unbid-den memories of slaughter and carnage and guilt. He had survived by sheer luck. Chance had saved him. But for what? To have the only woman he ever loved stolen from him?

'I was there. They call it the Battle of Shiloh now, I hear.'

Jesperson slowly drained his glass then rested it on his knee.

'How long has she been gone?'

'Little under two years. I've been trailing her since. Not a lot to go on. Traders and settlers have passed on rumors. I've interviewed survivors at army posts in Oklahoma Territory, Texas, New Mexico. Last I heard was that Victorio had her. Traded for her.'

'Victorio is dead,' Jesperson said bluntly. In his voice there was a touch of disappointment. 'He didn't have a white woman with him when he was killed.'

Cantrell settled back against the desk, feeling himself grow suddenly tired. In the silence Garther took his glass and Jesperson's and refilled them. The lieutenant tried to offer Cantrell condolence with a sympathetic look but he felt like an intruder and quickly retreated to a corner of the room.

'When?'

'Last summer the Negro Ninth and Tenth Calvary chased Victorio out of Texas and into Mexico. The Texas Rangers continued the pursuit but were turned back by Colonel Joaquin Terrazas of the Chihuahua militia. He wanted the personal glory. Last October his regiment cornered Victorio in the Tres Castillas range about sixty miles inside Mexico. Terrazas and his men slaughtered much of the camp. They even killed women and children – Apache women and children. What was left of them didn't have any more fight in them.'

Cantrell pulled off his hat and stared down into the crown as he ran his fingers through his matted and tangled hair.

'Talk to the Indians, if you think it will do any good, Cantrell. You're welcome to spend the night. Garther will take care of what you need. I'm sorry the trail's dead.'

Cantrell forced himself to push off the desk and walk to the door. He was numb, head to toe. He had spent the better part of two years hunting, following rumors and stories, and now he had nothing. Nowhere to turn, and no hope of finding Mary. He knew what Jesperson wasn't saying. It was the same thing Cantrell had refused to admit for the better part of a year. More likely than not, Mary was dead.

Outside the sun was very low on the horizon. It bathed the camp in an orange glow.

'We could get you something to eat first,' Garther suggested. 'Get a good night's sleep and start questioning the captives in the morning.'

'Tonight,' was all Cantrell could say.

The men led their horses through the center of camp to the livery where Garther ordered the stableman to see to Cantrell's horse. Taking the man's saddle-bags and rifle, the lieutenant led Cantrell toward the east end of the camp where the makeshift pens stood. He called to a baby-faced private and handed off Cantrell's belongings.

'We've got officer guest-quarters open, I'll have you situated there.'

'Don't bother.' He felt angry all of a sudden, jarred by emotion from his lethargy. If Mary were dead there wasn't anything he could do about it. But he had to know and, if possible, find out who'd killed her. He owed her that much, and more.

'Put me with the enlisted, Private,' he told the uncertain youngster awaiting orders. 'I never made it past sergeant, and I'm a better man for it.'

Garther nodded to the private, who scurried off.

'I'll take you to the pens now.'

Torches had been lit around the outer rim of the pens, casting a wavering light but no heat on the captives. A dozen soldiers stood at attention yet glassy-eyed with boredom. Foolishly, to a man, they had their backs to the pens. Cantrell understood why. He had no reason to love Indians but felt sorry for these. Crowded as they were, dirty, with only a small sack of belongings to mark their lives, they were a pathetic band. No longer a powerful enemy, they had been utterly destroyed. Thankfully, the children were asleep, and they looked like all sleeping children – innocent and peaceful.

The guard on the gate saluted as Garther approached

and lifted the single bar that formed the barrier between freedom and captivity.

'Good luck,' Garther said.

Cantrell took a deep, steeling breath and stepped into the pen. As he did, he pulled from his shirt pocket a scratched and dulled gold locket. There had been a chain at one time but he'd lost it along the way. With reverence he clicked open the lid and angled the revealed face to catch the light. Mary. She was alive in that picture. Bright and strong, her chin pushed out slightly, her eyes twinkling, holding a smile. Her long hair had been bundled up in a thick knot, lifted off her neck. A willful strand had fallen back to lightly caress her nape.

He felt hollow looking at her, missing her.

The captives didn't react to him. They ignored his approach, and when he knelt beside an old grandmother he was ignored. He moved among them like a ghost. When he showed the locket and the picture of Mary none looked at it. Deeper into their midst he went, growing more frustrated with each empty stare.

'Please, mother,' he said, taking hold of one woman's arm. He had picked up a few words of Apache over the past couple of years, but not enough to use in conversation. She turned toward him, her gaze blank and uncaring. 'I just need to know,' he pleaded.

Her sudden glance away betrayed her. Now he felt other eyes on him and the heat of someone crowding close. He looked up sharply to find himself ringed by old men and women glaring hotly at him and inching nearer. He started to rise when the old woman grabbed his forearm in a steely grip and pulled mightily. Losing his balance he dropped to one knee, wobbling as he tried to keep his feet under him. Angrily he clawed at her leathery fingers.

Dropping the locket, he swept his hand back to the Colt hanging from his hip. Hands slapped at his arm, keeping him from the gun. He tried to rise again, got half-way, then stumbled as a heavy body shoved against him. Tumbling, he caught himself before he flattened against the ground. A bright pain exploded in his ribs suddenly. He opened his mouth to cry out but the shock of it had taken his voice.

Wearily, he again tried to rise. His knees buckled under the weight of the bodies pressing down on him. He was cold now and blind and he let himself sink deep into the blackness that closed in around him.

CHAPTER TWO

'Sorry, Cantrell, but looks like you ended up in officer's quarters after all.'

Slowly, he opened his eyes, squinting, blinking away the grit that glued them shut. It was day and yellow sunlight streaked in through a dirty window to his right. Morning, he thought. Lifting his head he saw a small table with a lamp and a writing-box. Two worn chairs rested against the opposite wall. The room was otherwise bare.

Garther stood beside the bed framed in the muted glow of light coming in through the window.

'What happened?' Cantrell asked, his voice croaking.

'You were knifed. One of the captives had a weapon and decided you needed a hole in your chest.' Reflexively, Cantrell lifted his hand to his chest, gently probing. He felt a bandage and, although the area was a little tender, there wasn't much pain. 'Who ever attacked you wasn't very good. They hit you a glancing blow and didn't do much more than scratch you. When you fell you got stuck again, though. Took about a half inch of skin out of your side.'

'I don't feel. . . .'

'You wouldn't. The sawbones gave you something for

the pain. You've had a fever most of the night.'

Gingerly, Cantrell touched his left side and found another bandage. He wondered if the old woman had really wanted him dead, or if she had simply struck out. A way of counting coup, like a brave. Surely she'd had time to kill him if she had wanted to.

'How'd you know I was in trouble?'

'I was watching. When I lost sight of you I figured I'd better get in there. Good thing I did. You see who did this to you?'

Cantrell shook his head. 'There were too many of them.'

Garther nodded, unconvinced. 'Uh-huh.'

Pushing himself up on one elbow Cantrell grunted, 'I'd like to go back and try again.'

'Figured you might, so I asked. Colonel says no. You're to recover and, when you're ready, leave. He wants no trouble with these Indians and he figures that's all you'll bring.'

Settling back against the pillow, Cantrell asked, 'So, friend, you've been my nurse all night?'

'Not me.' He looked at Cantrell with a sly smile. 'And to tell you the truth, she was wasted on you. I'll send her in with breakfast. Maybe later you'll feel like telling me the truth about which captive tried to butcher you.'

Grinning, Garther tossed a wave and walked out of the room.

Cantrell pushed back against the pillow and wriggled a bit to get it into a comfortable position behind his head. He let himself sink into the soft mattress and absorbed the crisp, clean feel of the sheets. How long had it been since he'd slept on sheets? He couldn't remember and was glad he couldn't. Mary had kept a fine house and they'd had sheets on their bed, a bed Cantrell had built himself. That was all gone now, burned to the ground and the ashes scattered to the winds. He no longer remembered the feel of those sheets on his skin. He couldn't remember the feel of Mary on his skin any more, either.

He dozed for a while and when he awoke the sun had moved out of the window. Feeling a sudden anger, he swung his legs over the side of the bed and sat up. His pants hung over the back of a chair with his saddle-bags lying on the seat. His Winchester in its fringed buckskin sheath leaned up against the wall. He didn't see his shirt, but that didn't matter. He had a spare in the saddle-bags.

'Where do you think you're going?'

Cantrell pivoted on his seat too quickly, sending a spike of pain cutting through his chest. He grunted, scowling. A woman stood in the doorway holding a tray.

'See,' she said with considerable superiority, 'you shouldn't be moving.'

'And you shouldn't be sneaking up on a man and screeching at him.'

With light movements she swooped into the room, placed the tray down on the table, and got behind Cantrell, who had begun to sway. She caught him and eased him back onto the pillow, then helped him lift his legs back onto the bed. Quite motherly, she adjusted his covers, pulling them down to his waist.

'Lady!' Cantrell complained, taking hold of her wrists as she reached for his bandages. The wound had opened and fresh blood discolored the dressing on his chest.

'Mr Cantrell, I have seen it all before.'

'Not on me you haven't.'

'Yes, you. The fort doctor is out with Company E on a sweep of the valley. It was either me being your nurse, or the cook.'

Cantrell looked at her narrowly. She'd made good bandages, he admitted grudgingly. He wasn't dead, so she must know a bit about doctoring. Reluctantly, he let his hands drop and allowed her to touch him.

She moved silently and with practiced authority, to remove the bloody square of white cloth. She was none too gentle. He watched her get up and go to the desk, pour water out of a pitcher into a bowl, and return to him. She didn't look at him, concentrating deeply. He sensed anger in her and recognized the smell of desperation about her. It was a scent with which he was very familiar.

She wasn't a tall woman, but she held herself erect and proud. Her hazel eyes were clear and sharp and big and round. They seemed huge, deep. She wore her long chestnut hair parted on the side and swept over one shoulder. Even in the room's dull light it gleamed. She had delicate features and clear, pale skin. Her dress was sturdy, a dark blue with yellow striping like an army uniform, complete with large brass buttons. A traveling dress, but one that couldn't hide the inviting shape that lay within.

When she had finished replacing the bandages she went to the window, opened it, and tossed out the bloodied water.

'You're a pretty good patient,' she said, 'when you're not talking.'

'Thanks. Do I get to know your name?'

She brought the tray to Cantrell and set it in front of him. Then she helped him into a sitting position. The tray had a heaping plate of eggs, toast, a pot of coffee, and half

23

a dozen strips of bacon.

'My name is Susan Covington.'

'Much obliged, Mrs Covington.' Cantrell began shoveling eggs into his mouth.

Susan reached over and poured coffee for him.

'Then Lieutenant Garther told you something of me?' she asked with veiled curiosity.

'Uh-uh. Figured you were married because there aren't many women out here who aren't. And none attached to army forts that aren't. Besides, you're new to the country.'

She could not hide her surprise. 'And why would you say that?'

'A desert woman shows some sign of weather on her features. You don't. And that dress is fine for traveling, but you can't work in it. Not out here.' He glanced up at her and thought she might have been offended. But she looked at him squarely, a bit of amusement on her face. 'If you don't mind my saying, ma'am,' he added.

'Not at all, Mr Cantrell. You are right, of course. I'm from the East. I've come to find my husband. I've word he might be dead.'

Cantrell put down his fork and pushed the tray away.

'He was stationed here?'

'That is unclear.' She stood up, very stiff now, and spoke in a clipped tone. 'Colonel Jesperson has been less than helpful, and I don't really understand how the army conducts its business.'

Odds are, Cantrell thought, he was being more helpful than she realized. Trying to spare her some dark truths about war with the Indians.

'If he died out here, ma'am, you won't recover his body. If the Indians got to him, you won't want to find him.'

24

That made her bristle with shock and annoyance. Her face whitened then flushed with an angry red.

'Thank you for your bluntness, Mr Cantrell. It is certainly refreshing. But I intend to find my husband, be he dead or alive. I understand we share a similar sentiment.'

Without waiting for a reply she turned on her heels and strode out of the room. Cantrell let out a slow whistle before returning to his breakfast.

He rested all that day, dozing now and again. He found fresh bandages on his chest and wrapped around his side when he awoke close at suppertime and knew Susan had visited him. A private brought his meal, saluting awkwardly, unsure of Cantrell's status. Toward evening he heard a couple of small children nearby, giggling, playing until they were hushed and sent scurrying away. Two caissons rolled by, their heavy wheels crunching alongside the echoing tread of marching soldiers. A bugle sounded the bright, staccato call *To The Colors*. Cantrell lay in his bed and envisioned the flags being lowered for the night. Two cannon spat with a whipsaw crack and Cantrell could see the flicker of light from the parade ground through his window as the charges fired. The color-guard marched off, leaving the cannon behind. In the quiet that followed the plaintive sound of *Taps* drifted through the fort.

Cantrell had slept too much during the day. He grew restless, frustrated with sleeplessness. He found himself hoping that Susan would come in and talk to him, then immediately felt guilty. She had her own problems, ones Cantrell understood well. The truth was they were both looking for ghosts. Cantrell knew that, even if Susan didn't. Their spouses were gone. Dead. There was no need to keep on looking for them. Except both he and Susan would not quit.

He smiled thinking of her scrappy behavior, how determined she was to find her man. He admired her, too. But also he felt a pang in his gut. She would have to come to the same realization Cantrell had reached. Soon enough, she would.

When he awoke the next morning energy had returned to his muscles. His body fairly quivered with the desire to get up and move. Gingerly he removed himself from bed and tested his wounds. The damage to his chest was minimal and was already healing. He pulled off the bandages and slipped on his spare shirt. He was more careful getting into his pants. The gash on his side was deeper and more painful. Looking at in the mirror, though, it appeared to be healing well and clean.

He found spare bandages on the desk where Susan had left them the day before and used these to redress his side wound. That done he finished dressing, gathered his belongings, and left the room. There were no guards about but the camp was actively in full swing. Cantrell had slept through *Reveille* and the morning *To The Colors* and no doubt had missed breakfast. He thought of Susan only in that she hadn't brought him his meal. His rumbling stomach was his immediate concern.

Two troopers quickstepped toward him, intent on some destination. They ignored him and kept marching.

'Just want to know where the mess is,' Cantrell said.

One of the troopers called over his shoulder, 'Down Cannon Alley, across the parade ground and on your right. Follow the burned smell.'

'Obliged.'

26

*

Susan Covington had eaten breakfast with the kitchen help in the mess hall as she had done each of the five days since her arrival. Colonel Jesperson had been kind enough, but it was clear that he did not want her in camp. There were few women here, maybe ten, and most of those were Indians. This was not a safe place, he told her often. It wouldn't be until the Indian problem had been settled.

She cared little for his Indian problem. She wanted only to find her husband, or his body. Garther and the others in Jesperson's command had been sympathetic, but not very helpful. Three days ago a corporal had come to her with word from Garther that her husband had been reposted to Fort Wingate as a replacement. William, her husband, was a lieutenant and commanded a patrol on a relief mission to the fort. This made little sense to Susan who found everything the army did frustrating.

Susan had been given quarters while she awaited word from her husband. To pay her way, she served breakfast each morning in the soldiers' mess and nursed for the doctor whenever he needed help. Following breakfast she would go to Jesperson's office and wait outside until he agreed to see her. He would grumble the same platitudes each morning and implore her to go home and await word from her husband or the army. She hated him for this, his refusal to be honest with her. In her heart she felt that William was dead. She just wanted Jesperson to tell her so. Still, there was a small beat of hope in her breast, and so she haunted the colonel, praying for an answer.

Most of the soldiers were gone, and Susan was collecting plates in a metal tub, when Cantrell walked in. She flushed with anger for an instant seeing him out of bed, but his swaggering stride convinced her immediately that he had healed well enough. Besides, he wasn't her concern.

'Good morning,' he mouthed from across the cavernous hall. Approaching her she saw that he did favor his left side just a bit. That wound was the deeper of the two. It was sure to hurt still.

'You needn't have taken your entire kit,' she said when he stopped in front of her.

'When it's all you've got, you keep it close,' he told her. 'Any chance of getting some breakfast?'

She turned to peer into the kitchen. 'Looks like they've taken away the bowls. Sit down, I'll try to rustle up something for you.'

Ten minutes later she returned with a meal much like she'd served him the previous day. It was good and he wasted no time finishing it.

'Thought you might drop by this morning,' he said.

'Several patrols returned last night. The kitchen was busier than usual. Looks like you were able to take care of yourself.'

Cantrell dipped his head. 'Figured I'd chased you off.'

'Because of the opinion you expressed? Believe me, Mr Cantrell, I do not wilt because of a man's opinion.'

He grinned. 'No. I didn't figure you did.'

'If I did, I would already be on my way back to Maryland and not hounding Colonel Jesperson. How are those bandages?'

'Just fine. Changed them before I left.'

'I guess you'll be leaving the fort now.'

Cantrell shrugged. 'Don't know what else to do. I've been chasing a man for nearly a year only to find out that he's dead and probably never even saw my wife. I can't ask him anything now, and those captives in the yard out there aren't about to tell me a thing. I guess I could try again.' Staring down at his coffee cup he told her of his wife, their life together in Texas, of her capture, and his two-year hunt. The image of his burned home, nothing but ashes and a single charred post sticking out of the ground in what had been the main room of their house, was vivid in his mind. Everything had been destroyed, either by fire or by the savage attack. He had found only a single dinner-plate intact. Mary's best china. It had somehow survived the wanton devastation and the blaze set by the Apaches. With crude sticks he had built a shelf and strapped it to the post, making a rough mantel on which he gently rested the plate. It was the last thing he had done before saddling his best horse and racing off in pursuit. In the two years he had been on her trail, following rumors and whispers, he'd found nothing of her or of those who had taken her.

'Try again,' Susan said. Cantrell looked up to find her watching him intently with deep, almost desperate eyes.

'Maybe we should both try again.' He stood and held out his hand to her. Smiling wanly, Susan took it and rose beside him. She paused to take off her long apron and adjust her hair then walked with him out of the mess hall.

They were silent until they reached Jesperson's office.

A corporal stood guard outside the office door. A rifle a little too large and too heavy rested like an anvil on his shoulder. He snapped to attention at their approach and his face tightened.

'The colonel respectfully requests you await his return,

Mrs Covington.' With a sharp quarter-turn the corporal shoved the office door open. 'There is a pot of coffee on the table, ma'am. The colonel should return shortly.'

That her visit had been planned for brought a flush of annoyance to her face. Cantrell grinned, knowing the old fox had countered Susan's persistence with an army stonewall.

Cantrell made himself at home in Jesperson's office and poured coffee for the both of them. They didn't have long to wait before the colonel entered the room. His demeanor was easy to read. Stiff, stepping boldly, he marched in and took the chair behind his desk. He did not make eye contact with Susan. Cantrell's stomach tightened knowing instinctively the news he brought.

A moment later a big-chested sergeant entered the room, snapping to attention just over the threshold. Seeing Susan, he swept the torn and dusty cap from his head and began kneading it with thick, nervous fingers.

'Why are you here, Cantrell?' Jesperson growled.

Before he could answer, Susan spoke up. 'I asked him to join me, Colonel. I knew you wouldn't mind.'

'What? Yes? Well, it doesn't much matter.' Jesperson nodded to the sergeant, who stepped forward, clearly uncomfortable. 'Mrs Covington, I've asked you many times since your arrival to go home and await word from the army. Well, word has come, finally, and I'm sorry. Sergeant Valendez can supply you with the information you seek. He came in with one of the patrols early this morning. After he has satisfied you, I hope you will heed my advice and return home. In two days there is a supply train going south which will take you to Edgerton where you will be able to book passage on a train heading east to the Texas coast.'

Bristling at his abrupt manner, Susan pivoted toward the fidgeting sergeant and said, 'You have news of my husband? Of William Covington?'

'Beggin' yer pardon, ma'am, but I do.' He swallowed hard, his eyes locked on hers. 'I was one who buried him.'

Cantrell watched Susan control her emotions as she swayed slightly on her feet. With a deep breath she steeled herself and nodded for the sergeant to continue.

'He was on patrol in the Zunis and he and Private Stovall got separated from the rest. An Apache raiding party cornered 'em in a box canyon and, well, done for them. Reinforcements got there too late.' He swallowed again then added, 'I'm awful sorry ma'am. He died fighting, though.'

'Cold comfort, Sergeant.'

From behind his desk Jesperson said, 'My condolences as well, madam. The army has lost a very good officer.'

Icily, Susan said, 'Thank you, Colonel. How is it that Sergeant Valendez so conveniently brings news of my husband?'

Jesperson snorted gruffly. 'Convenient it was not, madam. When you and Mr Cantrell arrived within hours of each other, both of you with similar questions, I dispatched a rider to Fort Wingate. The sergeant returns as a result of my enquiries. I regret, Mr Cantrell, that I have no news for you.'

'Didn't expect any.'

'Colonel, have you my husband's effects?'

'They were not brought here. They'll be sent from Fort Wingate to your home. It will take some time, however. You should be home far in advance of the shipment.'

'Yes, Colonel. I'm sure I will be. How do I reach Fort Wingate?'

Jesperson leapt out of his chair and shook a fist at Susan. 'Now look here, madam, this territory is no place for a woman to be casually traveling through.'

'I assure you, Colonel, there is nothing casual about my travels. Sergeant, my husband is buried at Fort Wingate, you say? Then I want to go there and see his grave.'

'Ma'am . . .' The sergeant nervously eyed Jesperson.

'It is not that I distrust you, Sergeant. Of that you may be sure. It's just . . . I have to see it for myself. I hope you understand.'

'It doesn't damn matter what the sergeant understands, your going to Fort Wingate is out of the question. Please, Mrs Covington, go home.'

'I will not.'

'This is dangerous country, madam. Do you think that your husband would want you to risk your life just to see his grave?'

'My husband is beyond caring about such things, Colonel. I am going.'

'If you do, it won't be with the help of this man's army. Good-day.'

'That you think you've been of any help at all is quite amusing, Colonel. Good-day to you.'

Cantrell hesitated, a grim smile cracking his rough face, before he turned to follow Susan Covington out of the office.

'Blast it, Cantrell, can't you do something with her?'

'I'm on her side, Colonel.' Glancing at the still-fidgeting sergeant, Cantrell asked, 'Was Covington killed with rifle or bow and arrow?'

32

Blanching, the sergeant said, 'Neither. They done for him with a hatchet.' Cantrell's stomach turned over once as he pictured the corpse. 'Weren't a pretty sight, sir. Nothin' a wife should see.'

'Nor,' Jesperson added, 'should she know about it.'

'Not knowing the truth could get her killed, Colonel.'

Jesperson slumped back into his chair. 'No one back home should ever know what happens in war, Reb. You know that. Hell, I can tell by looking at you that you live by that rule. How many people have you told about what you saw at Shiloh? Hmm? About what you had to do? No, I didn't think so. You probably didn't even tell your wife. War is a bloody cruel thing and it was never meant to be shared with . . . proper people.'

Cantrell tried to muster hatred for the colonel but he couldn't. The soldier was right. Some things you just didn't talk about. You spared the good people and your loved ones and fought the demons all alone. The ones with terrified eyes and the ones that begged you for just one more second of life.

'Talk to her, Cantrell. Get her to go home. And go home yourself. There's nothing more you can do.'

Susan waited for him on the dusty street, pacing with pent-up rage. She looked up sharply when he came out, then spun on her heels and began stalking back toward the guest-quarters.

'Susan, wait.'

He caught her lightly by the arm, feeling her soft warmth beneath the sheer organza of her sleeve. She stopped without looking at him.

'It was bad, Susan,' he said, his voice cold and distant. 'He died in pain. The Apache used a tomahawk on him.'

He could feel her trembling. Her face got pale and her eyes began to glisten with tears. He held onto her arm thinking she would faint. When she didn't he let go and she turned to him.

'Will you take me to Fort Wingate? I mean to go, and if you won't I will find someone who will take me.'

Cantrell cast a rueful eye back toward Jesperson's office. When he looked again at Susan a half-smile played on his face.

'I'll take you, Mrs Covington. I'll get you to Fort Wingate.'

CHAPTER THREE

They made conspicuous plans to leave the following morning. Colonel Jesperson provided a horse and saddle for Susan, apologizing that he had no buggy or wagon to spare as the supply train was not ready to leave. They would have food and water, though, and Cantrell was told he could stock up on ammunition if he was running low. The colonel wanted them gone, as fast as they could travel.

That night Cantrell and Susan ate at the mess-hall, keeping to themselves, silent as conspirators. Cantrell had decided that he would try to get as much food as they could carry for their long trek north. They needed a pack-horse, but he didn't think he could get one without the Colonel getting wind of it. They'd have to make do on the two animals they had.

Night fell slowly on the desert. The high clouds caught the sun's deep orange and red colors, shaded them with charcoal, and blanketed them in a rich veil of blue. Taking their time, Cantrell and Susan walked back to their rooms. Cantrell had spun a cigarette out of a pack of papers and a bag of tobacco from his shirt-pocket and slowly smoked it.

'I was very cruel to him,' Susan said, her voice little

more than a sigh.

Reveille had been blown, the cannons had been fired. The air was still, quiet. Cantrell said nothing. If she wanted to speak, she would.

'We had it very comfortable in Baltimore. But William wasn't happy. He wanted to leave his mark, achieve . . . something. Before the frontier was gone. I didn't understand.' She huffed out a small, humorless laugh. 'What wife would understand her husband's desire to go off and kill. Perhaps to be killed. And for what? Look at them.'

Susan pointed toward the pens where the Indian captives were kept. There were only a few in them now. The hundred or so from the previous day had already begun their long, desperate march west.

'They're a beaten people,' Susan said, her voice trembling slightly. 'He died for nothing.'

They came to her door and she paused. 'Mr Cantrell, I'm sorry. I should never have asked you to help me. You have your own quest and it's just as important as mine.'

He smiled weakly. 'You're not keeping me from it. I don't have anywhere else to go. No other place to check for my wife. If she's still alive.' Susan's face softened and she reached out to touch his arm. He was lost, she realized, and despondent. 'They're moving Indians through Fort Wingate, too, so I'll go up there with you and ask around.'

Leaning against his chest she reached up and kissed Cantrell's cheek.

'Thank you, Mr Cantrell. I'll be ready at first light.'

She slipped through her door and closed it behind her, the warmth of her still fresh on his face.

Restless, Cantrell turned from the housing row and

made his way to the center of the parade ground. Two sentries cast quick glances toward him as he passed. Neither was old enough to shave, let alone carry a gun. Yet here they were in hostile territory protecting a regiment of men with two Enfields.

Building another smoke, Cantrell continued north and let his mind wander. Ahead were the corrals in which the Indians were kept. Two more sentries stepped forward as he neared and lowered their rifles.

'Can't let you any closer, sir.'

This one wasn't a boy. He carried his big frame with confidence and strength. A canny corporal who had clearly seen his share of action. His eyes darted to Cantrell's hip and showed only the slightest relief when he didn't see a gun holstered there. Cantrell had returned his things to his room before going to supper with Susan.

Cantrell shrugged. 'Just out for a walk, soldier. Not even armed.'

'Yes, sir. I'm glad for that. But the colonel says you're not to go near the Indians.'

'My wife. . . .'

'I know,' the man said. 'And I'm sorry. The colonel doesn't want you attacked again.'

'All right, Corporal.' He hadn't expected to discover anything, but he had to try.

'Sir.' The big corporal stepped forward and brought his voice low. 'I asked them about a white woman. I know a little Apache, you see, and figured you'd want to know.'

Cantrell's heart squeezed a bit in his chest. 'And what did they say?'

The corporal shook his head. 'They haven't seen a

white woman in a long time. And they never had a captive with them.'

Cantrell nodded. Until that moment he hadn't realized just how much he'd hoped to learn some news.

'Thanks, Corporal.'

Night had fallen dark and cool as Cantrell slowly made his way back to his quarters. He rolled another cigarette to give his hands something to do, then let it hang on his lip, indifferent to the thing. He had just passed the livery stable when a hand reached out of the darkness and grabbed his shirt-front.

Cantrell let himself roll into his attacker and brought his knee up sharply. The man had been expecting it, knocking away the blow with a slap of his hand. Off balance, Cantrell was spun about and grabbed by a strong arm around his neck. Another man stepped in front of Cantrell and pinned his arms.

'Keep it down, Cantrell,' a voice harshly whispered. 'It's Lieutenant Garther.'

Cantrell forced himself to relax, letting tension drain from his body. A moment later he was released. A match flared to life and in its dim halo he saw Garther's weathered face. Sergeant Valendez eased into the light, grinning sheepishly.

'Sorry, sir,' he mumbled.

'What's this about?'

'Quiet. Come here.'

Garther led them behind the stable, Cantrell moving warily, almost blindly in the blackened night. Safe behind the barn, Garther lit another match. The three crowded close together.

'You're going with Mrs Covington up to Fort Wingate.'

Cantrell shook his head. 'Got your information from a dry hole, Lieutenant. Told the colonel this afternoon that the lady and I are heading south for the train.'

'Well, you can head north for it, too, and the trip will be faster and easier. It crosses the river from the east about two days' ride from here. A lot safer, too.'

The match went out leaving them in the dark.

'I'll talk to the lady about it. I'm sure she won't care which way we head.'

'You'll go north. Only I don't figure you'll take the train. She wants to go to Fort Wingate and from what I've seen that's not a lady to be denied. But you'll want to go cross-country to keep looking for your wife.'

Anger welling up inside him, he asked, 'What do you want, Garther?'

'You'll be picking up three horses tomorrow morning. The extra one is a pack-horse. It's a long ride to the fort and you'll need the additional supplies. I'll see that you get an extra rifle and enough ammunition, too.'

'Why?'

'The colonel's not lying, Cantrell. He's told you and Mrs Covington the truth about her husband. That is, as far as it goes. He's dead, and it looks like Apaches killed him.'

'Looks like?'

'That's right.' Garther sparked another match to life and held it up between them. 'Valendez, tell him what you told me.'

Swallowing hard, Valendez said, 'The colonel didn't want me to tell the lady because there wasn't a thing she could do about it. I talked to some of the men who brought the lieutenant back to be buried. They didn't see no sign of an Indian raiding party. Just a couple of horses.'

'Two or twenty, what does it matter?'

'These horses was shod.'

The match had gone out again but Garther didn't light another one.

'Did these men you talked to report that to the post commander?' Cantrell asked, surprised to feel his throat constrict.

'They've got their problems, sir, like we do. Too many Indians, and they're down some men. They've no time for guesswork and maybes.'

Cantrell thought for a minute. He was suddenly in the middle of something of which he wanted no part. A deep weariness came over him. He knew there was nothing he would ever find out about his wife, knew that she was dead and gone. But he couldn't let go. There was in him an overwhelming urge to get back on the trail, even if it led nowhere. Yet he couldn't abandon Susan, either. She would stir up a hornet's nest at Fort Wingate and it might get her killed.

'You're telling me he was murdered.'

'I'm not telling you anything,' Valendez croaked.

From the dark, Garther added, 'Neither am I. I'm not giving you a pack-horse and a rifle, either.'

Cantrell felt more than heard the men move away from him. Then, from a few yards away, Garther spoke. 'Keep your eyes open, Cantrell. For the lady's sake and for yours.'

A moment later they were gone, leaving Cantrell alone with dark thoughts.

Susan felt a chilling wisp of air float past her face and her eyes opened. The small brazier in the corner came into focus, a black shadow among the deeper shadows of the room. A tiny red glow flickered in the pan. The night air lay cold and heavy on her despite the thick down comforter in which she had wrapped herself. The heavy wool curtains were drawn tight so no light got into the room.

There had been a sound. It had ridden into her quarters on the breath of iced morning air.

Careful to keep still, Susan continued with her breathing as if asleep. It sounded loud to her ear and false. Very slowly, she shifted her right hand.

Someone moved into the room. A floorboard creaked. Something brushed against the bed.

Susan's heart fluttered a furious beat. She felt herself growing angry, outraged, as she struggled to retain her composure.

The intruder sat on the bed, making the springs creak. She felt herself rolling slightly toward him. A hand touched her shoulder lightly, steadying her. Then she felt him lean over, his face hovering close to hers.

Throwing aside the covers, Susan flailed out with her left arm and slapped the man's nose. Blindly she grabbed an ear and yanked. He stifled a yelp as his head jerked around. With her right hand, Susan brought forth a revolver and placed the end of its short barrel in his eye socket.

'I do not need an explanation,' she said. 'Just leave.'

'Not without you,' Cantrell said.

Susan gasped and let go of Cantrell's ear. Slowly, Cantrell stood up. A moment later she heard him at the coals and saw new life breathed into them. A dull red glow lit part of the room.

He could see her now, half out of the bed, a feather-light nightgown twisted about her. Perceiving the danger past, she began to shiver, the heat of her anger no longer able to ward off the cold air. She held the gun loosely in hand. A thirty-eight, he saw in a glance. A McWorter.

'Mr Cantrell, I don't understand.'

'We need to leave now.'

'Why?'

He ignored her, turning to the window. He thrust back the curtains. In the distance the sky was purpling at the horizon. They still had a couple of hours until dawn. Less than that before the color-guard signaled the day's beginning.

'You don't have long to pack,' he said.

'I'm already packed.'

It was true. A valise and a bulging carpetbag sat on a chair by the door. Cantrell smiled.

'Good. That's very good. You've got warm clothes.'

'Yes.'

'Then get dressed. You can leave that thing you're wearing behind. It won't do any good where we're going. We'll take the blanket, too. I'll fold it up while you get into your clothes.'

Susan cocked an eyebrow and raised the gun slightly. 'Mr Cantrell, I am most certainly not getting out of this bed with you standing there. And I will not leave without proper preparations.'

'They're all made. Now get up.' Susan steadfastly refused. 'Mrs Covington, you said you would put yourself in my hands. Trust me to see you safely to Fort Wingate. If you can't obey me now, your stubbornness might get us killed later out on the road.'

'I obey no man,' she said, defiantly.

Cantrell held his anger in check, just barely. 'We have to leave the fort before Jesperson gets up. We have help from inside his command, but they won't be able to help us if we don't get away now.'

Susan hesitated a moment, thinking. She couldn't see Cantrell very well. His eyes were dark in shadows. He looked ominous rimmed in the red glow of the coals. She had put her trust in this man but wondered now if that had been the smart thing to do.

'And what of food, Mr Cantrell?'

'We'll eat on the road,' Cantrell said, his voice low and terse. 'We'll have plenty for the first few days. It'll be enough. Get up.'

She had more questions. Instead of asking them, she threw back the covers and unabashedly walked over to another chair holding her clothes. She dressed quickly, half-expecting Cantrell to watch her. Glancing over to him she saw him folding the comforter.

Within minutes she was ready. Cantrell waited by the door, his arms full. He nodded his satisfaction of her. She wore heavy wool pants and a wool shirt. He caught a glimpse of red long johns sticking out of the sleeve-ends and around the neck. Her boots were solid and heavy and she wore a thick sheepskin coat that draped half-way down her thighs. A new wide-brimmed hat sat back on her head. She wore it in its original style, with a rounded crown.

Her garb was not dissimilar from Cantrell's, but she wore it better. The clothing, cut for a man and tucked and pinched and stretched at the waist, hips, and chest, accentuated Susan's ample figure. Cantrell felt a sharp pain in his chest looking at her. His look soured and he knew

43

instantly that she had seen it.

'Won't this do?'

'You'll be fine.'

They hurried across the compound using light from a waning quarter-moon to find their way. They avoided the sentries and arrived at the stable after only a few minutes. The stableman greeted them sleepily but put up no argument when Cantrell called for his horses.

'Three?' Susan asked when she saw the stableman lead the animals out front.

'Later,' Cantrell said tersely.

He loaded the pack-horse and checked the wrapped package tied to the saddle. Garther had been true to his word. There was an extra Winchester and six boxes of shells. Cantrell checked the other sacks tied to the saddle to find a frying-pan, a coffeepot, some dried meat, and a few pounds each of coffee, sugar, flour, and some salt. Adding what he had collected in a late-night raid of the kitchens, Cantrell figured they had enough to get them to Wingate. If they didn't run into trouble and if they conserved.

'Let's go.'

Cantrell grabbed the reins of the pack-horse then climbed aboard his roan and started out of camp slowly. Susan followed on a black gelding that tossed its head wanting to run.

'You hold him in check,' Cantrell warned. 'We'll open them up in the daylight when we're far from here.'

Cantrell struck a course due north and within a few minutes found the wagon trail. The ground was packed solid, giving good, safe footing to the horses. The purple on the horizon had turned to blue with a pale band of yellow nudging its way skyward.

Cantrell knew the road, but not this far south. He had crossed the Rio Grand del Norte about a year ago and had wandered along the old Indian trail that had become a cattle trail when the whites started settling in the area. Now it was an army road, packed hard from the constant beat of iron-shod horses and wagon wheels. The cattle were gone, riding instead in long trains of Atchison Topeka & Santa Fe boxcars that paralleled the river. The only Indians to walk the road any more were captives being herded to new homes on unfamiliar reservations.

Soon, there was enough light to see by. They stopped and Cantrell surveyed the area. It was much the same as he had crossed several days before, making his way up from El Paso. The land was flat except for the occasional rolling hill. Scrub-brush and tufts of grass spotted the sunwashed sand. There were ground-cactus here and there, and in the shady places where water gathered stood a few stunted oak. Dry arroyo beds and deeper canyons cut the ground in ragged, angry gashes, suggesting water had been plentiful at some distant time. Now, only the river brought water; the river and the few streams that trickled out of the snowcapped mountains to the east and west, invisible in the haze of morning.

Cantrell turned in his saddle and looked back along the trail. No one was following. They were more than an hour out of Fort Craig. Maybe four miles gone. He didn't think that Jesperson would care which way they had gone, but he didn't want to take the chance. The colonel had no jurisdiction over civilians, but he had plenty of big men with guns. He'd get his way if push came to shove.

'Let's air these critters out,' Cantrell said. 'Looks like

45

yours is itching for a run.'

Susan smiled. 'I think he is at that.'

Together they broke into a fast canter and kept the pace up for a good mile. Susan rode well, and Western style, too. She wasn't a shy one, that's for sure, Cantrell caught himself thinking. At that moment she glanced at him and smiled again, her right eyebrow arching in challenge. Cantrell nodded and they both urged their mounts to a gallop.

Susan bent low over the gelding's mane, holding the reins short and rocking in perfect rhythm with the horse. She looked only ahead, the wind whipping her long hair and pulling at her hat-brim.

After a mile or so, Cantrell brought them down to a trot and finally to a slow walk. It was mid-morning when they stopped again to rest the horses and they had put a good fifteen miles behind them.

Noticing Cantrell checking their backtrail, Susan asked, 'You really think Colonel Jesperson will hunt us down for going north rather than south?' She had dismounted and was stretching the kinks out of her back.

'He might.'

'Then let's sell the horses first chance we get and take the train. There's a depot up ahead, isn't there?'

Cantrell loosened the cinches on his saddle then went over to Susan's mount and did the same. 'There is, but we can't sell the horses. Nobody'll buy a horse with an army brand. They'll figure them stolen, and nobody wants to cross the army.'

'Then we'll ride to Fort Wingate. He gave us the horses, didn't he? He can't object to us returning them to the army up there.'

'He might. Especially if he finds out we've got an extra horse and an army-issued rifle.'

'You stole a rifle?'

'Lieutenant Garther. He outfitted the pack-horse and gave us the gun and ammunition.'

'Why would he do that?'

Cantrell hitched the horses to some scrub-brush, loosely wrapping the reins around brittle clusters of twiglike branches.

'He knew we'd go north. Figured you wouldn't be denied.'

Her face flushed a little with embarrassment. 'Well, he was right.'

'Mrs Covington . . . he told me something else. It's not good. I think it might be better to turn back. I can still get you on a train headed East.'

Adamantly she shook her head. 'No, Mr Cantrell. I must see my husband's grave. I must make my peace with him.'

Cantrell turned away. 'It won't help.'

'You've not found your wife's grave, Mr Cantrell. You don't know that it won't help. Now please tell me why we should abandon our course.'

'Well, hell, it's mighty dangerous out here.' He waved an arm about angrily. 'Take a look out there. You don't see much of civilization, ma'am. And you won't. Not the whole trip. There are still Indians running loose. Not many, but enough renegades to make your scalp itch. Then there are the *bandidos*. The army's been hunting them down, and there's law about, but this is big country. A woman just isn't safe.'

'I have a gun, Mr Cantrell. In addition to being able to

47

draw it quickly and point, I can hit what I aim at.'

'Sure. But can you do it when they're shooting back. That's the trick.'

Susan stared at Cantrell for a moment and realized that he hadn't looked at her when he spoke. He was purposely avoiding her gaze.

'There's more, Mr Cantrell. Tell me. I have a right to know.' Her voice was strong, demanding. But her eyes were wide with a growing fear. She strained forward, willing Cantrell to talk. 'Tell me what it is.'

'Some think your husband wasn't killed by Apaches.'

Very softly she asked, 'Who, then?'

Cantrell shook his head, lifting his eyes to hers. 'I don't know. I gather from what they didn't say that it was a soldier, or more than one.'

'No.'

'I spoke with Sergeant Valendez last night, away from the colonel's hearing. He was at Fort Wingate, you'll remember. He had helped bury your husband. He's heard talk.' He went to her, taking her by the shoulders and pulling her face close to his. 'Listen, if that's what happened, then we'd be fools to go there. Let's get on a train and leave the territory. Back home you can petition your senator or the governor to look into these stories. You'll be safer.'

Susan pulled away from his grasp. 'It would be months, maybe a year before such an enquiry could be made. Don't you think that any evidence supporting that allegation would be erased?'

'Maybe,' he said with a deep sigh. 'But if a soldier did kill him, then the army doesn't want that out. They might kill to keep it quiet.'

Her face flamed with indignation. 'They wouldn't dare. I don't care what the danger . . . what are you looking at?'

Cantrell had moved away from the woman and was staring off to the north-east. Susan turned and followed his gaze. On a hill at the edge of their view a figure had skylined, hardly more than an elongated dot in the distance.

'What is it?'

As she asked, a second figure joined the first.

Cantrell shook his head. 'Could be anything.'

Slowly, he backed toward the horses. Finding the pack-animal he routed around in the bags tied to the saddle until he found the boxes of shells. These he took and put into his saddle-bags. Then he took the two spare canteens and wrapped the straps around his saddle horn. He freed the pack-horse from the bush, slapped its rump, and hurrawed it away, off the road.

'What are you doing?'

He tightened the cinches of her saddle and said, 'Get on.'

After tightening the cinches of his own saddle he mounted and turned the animals toward the hill. The dots were down off the ridge and invisible against the hard-packed sand. Only the trail dust they kicked up gave an indication of their presence. They were moving at a fast clip.

'Can you follow my lead?' he asked. 'Do what I say?'

She hesitated. 'I – Yes.'

'Stay to my left and a little behind me.' Cantrell checked the rifle in the boot to make sure it cleared the buckskin sheath cleanly. He looked at Susan, whose face was white. Her eyes were fixed on the approaching riders. 'You see that hill to the west? The one with the big rocks at its base?'

49

She turned her head, blinking, trying to focus on the new image. 'I see it.'

'It's about a mile. When I tell you, make a break for it and get behind those rocks.'

'Who are they?'

'I don't know. Braves, most likely. We'll ride slowly up the trail, like we haven't a care in the world. Can you do that?'

She took a long slow breath. Her chin quivered slightly. 'Yes.'

'Good. Let's go.'

CHAPTER FOUR

They moved out cautiously, keeping their horses to a slow walk. Neither of them took their eyes off the trail of dust rising softly into the warming air. The approaching riders were a mile away, or more, and coming on at a gallop. Cantrell thought he saw one of them carrying a lance. The light breeze brought a whisper of a sound: the thumping of horses' hoofs and a high-pitched yell.

The gelding whinnied and tossed its head. Fidgeting, it bumped up against Cantrell's roan, which craned its neck back and snapped at the black horse. Susan shortened up on the reins and leaned forward over the mane, whispering gentle words to comfort her mount.

Cantrell glanced out to the west. They had gone a little more than a hundred yards up the road and had a clear path to the western hill and its protective base of rock. Susan eyed him anxiously, letting her tongue sweep over her lips. Again he pulled at his rifle to make sure it cleared easily. The riders had not checked their speed.

'On my mark, Susan.' He glanced over his shoulder and saw her gaze was fixed on the riders who were now no more than a mile away. 'Do you hear me?'

She nodded sharply.

'Look to the hills, Susan.' Reluctantly she turned her attention west. 'You see the rocks? See the path we'll take? It's direct.'

'Around those two boulders,' she said.

'That's right. Now get ready.'

Cantrell let the roan drop back slightly. He wanted to rap the gelding on the rump to spur it into a gallop.

'What's that?'

Susan was looking east again, toward the riders. They were Indians, as Cantrell had suspected. He could see them well enough now. Cantrell shifted his gaze to see a dark line of mounted men coming up over the distant ridge where he had first seen the Indians. A flicker of light sparkled and a moment later dust spurted up beside the galloping riders. One of the horses jumped to the left and slammed against the other animal, nearly sending both crashing to the desert floor. Dimly, Cantrell heard the crack of a rifle shot, and a few moments later another.

Their horses stumbled to a stop and both Indians looked about, uncertain.

'Now?'

'No! Don't move.'

Cantrell reached out and grabbed the gelding's reins, stopping both horses.

'This is our chance,' Susan protested.

'Don't move.'

A brassy, staccato sound drifted toward them. A bugle calling assembly. At once, one of the Indians broke away and renewed his charge toward Cantrell and Susan. The other Indian called out to the first but did not follow. Up on the hill a squad of four riders had separated from the others and began a charge down the slope.

'Stay here,' Cantrell said as he nudged the roan forward, off the road and toward the oncoming rider. He could hear the thunder of the hoofs clearly now and as that registered he could also hear the Indian's war cry.

Cantrell squared his shoulders and waited. A trickle of sweat ran down the back of his neck.

Close now, the Indian shifted the lance in his hand and brought it up above his head. The small sorrel he was riding was nearly played out, lathered at the withers and the haunches.

Like a flash flood, the Indian charged, his eyes red and his face twisted in hate. He was young, no more than twelve years old. When he was only fifteen feet away he let fly the lance, slamming the weapon's point into the desert only inches from the roan. Cantrell flinched at the sound of the crude iron head punching the hard ground.

The Indian flew by only inches from Cantrell then skidded to a stop and turned about. Another rifle shot cracked in the distance. Cantrell looked out to see two of the four new riders racing toward him. The other two halted to gather up the second Indian. All of them were soldiers.

Crying out again, the Indian kicked his mount into a gallop and charged at Cantrell's back. He barely had time to brace himself before the Indian sped by him, whipping something against his shirt-sleeve. Cantrell felt a bite and a sudden sting but ignored the pain. Ahead, the Indian stopped and turned his horse about to face Cantrell. He held a long knife above his head and screamed triumphantly. Then he threw the knife tip first into the desert floor.

Flanking him, the soldiers caught the young brave and dragged him out of the saddle. One of the soldiers snaked a rope around his neck and began dragging him back to the column, just now making its way down the hill. Walking backwards, stumbling, the Indian wouldn't take his eyes off Cantrell. He grinned devilishly and laughed.

A corporal reined up his buckskin in front of Cantrell and without a word got down and retrieved the knife. He examined it for a moment then handed it toward Cantrell. There was a thin red stain on the blade.

'I guess you earned this,' the corporal said. 'You were lucky.'

'If you say so.'

The corporal remounted the buckskin. 'We're bringing a band of these renegades in. A couple got away from us. I've got a doctor with us could take a look at that injury,' he said with a nod toward Cantrell's upper arm where the shirt had been sliced open just below the shoulder.

'No thanks. I'm fine.'

The captured brave fought against the rope now. One of the soldiers got down and began hitting the Indian and looping the rope around him several times. Cantrell looked off toward the hill. He could make out six more soldiers escorting several dozen Indians. Herding them, really, like cattle.

'I'd unwrap that brave,' Cantrell said. 'You'll only just inflame the others.'

'We'll do all right,' the corporal said, bristling.

'You've had trouble with two of them already. You don't want to get the others in a killing mood.'

The corporal chortled. 'They're just children and old women.'

Cantrell gently rubbed his side, remembering what an old woman had done to him. Biting his tongue, he shrugged and said, 'Then I won't keep you, Corporal.'

'Stick to the road, mister. There are still a few bands around and you and your woman don't want to be caught in the open alone. There's a town about a half-day's ride from here. It isn't much but you'll be safe there.'

Cantrell nodded curtly and watched the corporal retrieve the lance and ride away. It was lucky, he thought, that the fool was so close to Fort Craig. A day or two more on the trail and that young brave would have had his scalp.

'Your arm,' Susan said when he rode back to her.

'I'm fine.' He had gathered up the pack-horse and started them up the road again.

'It should be tended to.'

'We'll make camp soon enough. I'll do it then.'

Cantrell didn't want to talk. He felt something boiling up inside him, something he couldn't quite name, and decided to keep his mouth shut. That left Susan alone with her thoughts all afternoon. He didn't exactly know what those were but he could guess, stealing a glimpse of her face from time to time. He had felt the same guilt she was feeling, the guilt of those left behind. You know in your heart that it's foolish to think that way, but there it is and you can't shake it off. Friends had told him it would get easier with time, that the pain of it wouldn't sting so much. Well, it had been two years and it was harder today than it had been the night he'd come home to a burning house and a missing wife.

Rounding a bend, the road edged closer to the river that bubbled below them through craggy, shallow canyons. After a time they paused to water the horses, walking them down to a short pebbly beach at the river's edge. Later that day they came to a place where the land flattened and the Rio Grande seemed to sit on top of the hard desert. The Atchison Topeka & Santa Fe track crossed here over a low bridge before continuing its northward stretch. They stayed to the west of the tracks and were soon shadowed by the jagged swell of the foothills of the Magdalena Mountains.

Dusk lay thick and gray over them by the time they reached a flat stretch where a town rose up suddenly out of the sand. Cantrell slowed the animals to a walk and moved off the road, carefully eyeing the weather-worn buildings and jaundiced lamplight puncturing a dozen windows. The town didn't have much to recommend it. He noted three saloons and a cantina and what might have been a stable. The other few buildings looked empty, unused. All the light was coming from the saloons and cantinas. But he heard no sounds.

'We should stop in that town,' Susan said.

'It's bound to be a little rough.' He watched her as she cast an uncertain eye over the place. 'You much of a hand at using the sky for your roof?' he asked.

'I can manage. But we should get you medical attention for your arm.'

Cantrell had forgotten all about the slice the young brave had given him. He shrugged. 'I spotted a stream among the foothills. Spotted it earlier. Should make a good place to camp. I'll wash it out there. It'll be fine.'

Susan couldn't keep concern and confusion from her face.

'There are three saloons in town, all lit up,' he said, explaining his reticence to take her into the town. 'No one's laughing or singing or even talking loud which means the men in there will be a surly bunch. That town's

56

a dry hole, not much good for anything. So you've got surly men with nothing to do, no purpose in life. That's the meanest kind. If we go in there, there'll be shooting. Easier just to avoid trouble. We'll find it soon enough.'

Nodding her understanding, Susan nudged her gelding to follow Cantrell as he pushed his horse into a trot. They found the stream within a few minutes and set up camp behind a short ridge that blocked their view of the town. The stream trickled through their camp. Cantrell found enough dry brush and twigs to get a fire going before he ranged further in search of bits of timber. He returned after half an hour with an armload of thicker chunks of wood.

'Sit here,' Susan said, calling Cantrell to her side. She had the coffee-pot full of water on the fire to boil and some strips of cloth. He didn't argue with her, and allowed her to roll up his sleeve to expose the injury. It had already started healing with dried blood all around the wound. She soaked the cloth and gently cleaned the cut. She let it bleed a little, then pressed clean, dry strips of cloth against the wound and tied them in place.

'I guess you've had a little experience with injuries,' he commented, rolling his sleeve down and buttoning the cuff.

'Have two brothers and I grew up on a farm. I've seen a few cuts. Of course, you've fairly been a scratching post for Apaches these past few days.'

He grinned. 'I have at that.'

Susan poured the leftover hot water out then went to refill it with fresh, cold water. She had taken the foodstuffs off the saddle while he was out gathering wood and arranged them on a rock. She set about making coffee and

57

panbread. Cantrell watched her efficient, simple movements and felt a mix of emotions. For his two years on the trail no one had made his food. It was pleasant watching her work, but it also gave him a strange sense of not belonging.

She made coffee differently, preferring to add the grounds as the water came to a boil instead of starting cold. She had taken some lard and cornmeal from Fort Craig's kitchens and used these to make the panbread. Into a smaller pan she cut hunks of ham and began warming them.

'Looks like you were busy before we left,' he said.

'I made a few friends at the fort. This is the only ham, though. The rest is jerked beef and venison and bacon, and very little of that.'

The sounds and smells of cooking began to emanate from the fire-pit. Cantrell inhaled deeply. 'Let's eat it while we've got it.'

An odd disquiet fell over the camp after they finished eating and cleaned the pans. Cantrell had taken his bedroll and used it as a soft pillow against the backstop of his saddle. Night had fallen cold and clear and it was time to sleep. Neither one of them moved, sitting each on opposite sides of the small fire.

'My reputation shall be irretrievably damaged,' she said with a wry smile, 'if word were to reach Baltimore that I spent the night under the stars with a man not my husband.'

Cantrell's face darkened. 'Sorry about that, Mrs Covington.'

She laughed lightly. 'Don't be, Mr Cantrell. I'll survive. And it's not as if any of my friends are likely to stumble upon us out here.'

'No. Not likely.' A small grin crept onto his face.

'I wonder,' she offered hesitantly. 'It's somewhat cumbersome calling you by your family name. We are to be companions for a time, after all. I would like you to call me Susan, if you're comfortable with that.'

A tremor ran through him for just a moment. She was right, of course. But this intimacy was something he had avoided for two years. His hatred and anger toward his wife's unknown killers had kept him at arm's length from other people all that time. The lack of intimacy with anyone had allowed him to focus on his quest. In the space of just a few days all of that was beginning to crumble.

'All right,' he said, his voice little more than a hoarse whisper. 'My name's Tobias.'

She smiled warmly. 'I like it.'

Like a crack, she was up and rooting through the pile of supplies removed from the horses earlier. She came back with her bedroll and the blanket pilfered from the fort. She laid these out close to the fire and wriggled inside them. Cantrell stoked the flames a little and added three more large bits of dried wood before getting his own bedroll and settling in.

'Is it a long way to Fort Wingate?' Susan asked after a time.

'Yes. Longer if we stick to the roads.'

'And you don't want to take the train?'

Cantrell shrugged. 'My funds are a bit low at this point.'

'I have money, Tobias.'

'I suppose if we stop at a good-sized town, one with a marshal, we could surrender the horses to him and sell the roan. That might work. Be a sight faster, too.'

'And safer?'

She had only experienced a taste of the violent life in Indian country but the worry was plain in her voice.

'It's safer,' he said. 'You'll need your rest. It's still another day's ride or two before we reach a town of any size.'

A light rain hampered their travel the next day. They passed two towns, both too small to have a town marshal. Still, both had tiny depots and, Cantrell figured, a train might stop occasionally to deliver mail or the odd passenger.

They didn't see another Indian and the road had little traffic. A fast-wheeling Conestoga stage rolled by in a cloud of dust, the driver eyeing them suspiciously until it passed. The shotgun rider turned on the bench seat to peer back along the road, watchful and wary. They passed a rider a few hours later. The man hesitated after spotting Susan and Cantrel, then, with his hand resting on the heavy butt of the gun at his hip, urged his horse into a canter. Pulling Susan off to the side Cantrell noticed the horse was carrying a heavy load: two burlap sacks tied to the saddle horn.

He nodded to the rider who perfunctorily tilted his head with a sharp thrust, then stared straight ahead. Susan watched the man go by, a puzzled look of disappointment on her face.

'People haven't been very friendly,' she said.

'Things are kind of wild out here, even with the army so close. There are still plenty of Indians making war and if it isn't them it's outlaws robbing stages and trains and others.'

'Travelers? Like us?'

'It happens. You've heard of Billy the Kid.'

'Yes, Tobias,' she said with barely disguised impatience. 'Even all the way back in Baltimore. I understand they killed that poor boy a few months ago.'

'Poor boy?' Cantrell squeezed a lid on his exasperation. He'd heard too many people speak well of the Kid even though he was a cold-blooded killer. 'Well, that "poor boy" was tame compared to some folks out here.'

They found an outcropping of rock around noon and stopped to eat. Wedged into the side of the hill, the rock formed a small canopy above them. Cantrell rode up the hill to get his bearings while Susan made coffee. Short cottonwoods dotted the edge of the river meandering off a ways to his right. Below him the single railroad track shot to the horizon straight and true. It looked lonely amid the tufts of grass and low mounds of hard-packed earth. He saw nothing ahead or behind. Yet he felt something niggling the back of his neck. No eyes were spying him but something was making the small hairs stand up and he couldn't put his finger on it.

Susan was right. Taking the train would be wiser. He hadn't wanted to in hopes of meeting up with wandering Indians. He knew what Sergeant Valendez had told him was correct. Mary was surely gone by now. But he couldn't bring his heart to yet believe that. He didn't want to pass up any chance to ask questions about her. Shaking his head, he realized a morbid fascination had gripped him. Rather than expecting to find her alive, he wanted to know - good or bad - what her last days and hours had been like. He wanted in some small way to share her experience, if not her fate.

Susan did not speak when he returned. She glanced at him several times as she poured coffee and fried up bacon. While he was gone she had unsaddled her horse and ground-hitched it near a thick clump of rabbit-grass. After a while he found himself watching her. Being an Eastern woman, he imagined that she was more accustomed to being served, not serving. She had adapted well to Western ways and the open trail. It was not something anyone could do. Sleeping on the ground, eating the same meager fare meal after meal, and spending long hours in the saddle was physically demanding and mentally draining. Susan did not complain. She seemed filled with a grim determination that was lightened by a childlike sense of adventure that played across her face and brightened the lilt in her voice.

Brooding, as he often did, he found a stark contrast between himself and Susan. He had never been conscious before of his dour expression and his bleak appearance. He had let his clothes go almost to ruin. His hat had been mercilessly battered. His boots barely hung together. The clothes on his back were filled with dirt and grime. But it was his face, drawn and lifeless, and the emptiness in his pale-blue eyes that told the story of a man slipping into oblivion. He had seen his reflection once, in a mirror back at the fort, and the apparition he spied in that glass haunted him now.

Yet he had smiled a little with Susan. Had felt himself stir to life, sensing in her a kindred spirit. Not just someone who shared his misery, but someone who understood his plight. His failure.

Finishing his coffee he looked up at Susan. She had already finished packing up again and was stamping out the small fire she had built.

'You'll do to ride with,' he said.

She flushed vividly. 'Thank you, Tobias.' She kicked around the ashes and poured water onto them, sending up a thin stream of smoke. 'My family owns a farm. It's not like farms out West. It's quite large and we have many people who work it. But my father believed in being able to take care of oneself on the land, so he taught all of us how to do that.'

'Your brothers?'

'An older sister, too. He taught us all to shoot and make a fire and care for the land.'

Cantrell nodded. His father had done much the same for him and his two brothers.

'He's gone now, your father?'

'Yes. A few years ago.'

Cantrell shook out his coffee-cup, then slipped it into the flour-sack strapped to the pack-saddle that contained their few cooking- and eating-utensils. He nodded toward Susan's saddle lying on the ground.

'He teach you to saddle a horse, too?'

'Yes,' she said. 'But I . . . well, Western saddles are quite a bit heavier than the saddles I'm used to. I don't know if I can throw it onto the horse.'

'Couldn't do it myself until I was sixteen,' Cantrell admitted. 'I was kind of scrawny up until then. My brothers gave me a time about it.'

'You've grown some since then,' she said. Her eyes widened suddenly and she turned away, her face flushing again.

Cantrell ignored her embarrassment. 'Yes, ma'am. That was my year. Got my brothers back in spades.'

Ten minutes later they were back on the trail. That nagging feeling came back to Cantrell and he began scouring the distance for signs of trouble. Susan noticed a change in his manner and watched him carefully, silently.

The Magdalena range closed in on them, tumbling in crumbling rocky chaos eastward toward the road. The railroad tracks emerged from between long rolling mounds of hillside and crossed the road as it angled toward a town. With dusk rising about them it was difficult to tell the town's size.

Cantrell brought them to a stop. He could see a number of low-lying adobe structures and what looked like a fairly good-sized train-depot. A stagecoach rumbled south toward them.

'Do you think we'll go into town?' Susan asked as the coach passed, the driver nodding curtly to them.

'Maybe so,' Cantrell said. 'I've been thinking about the train. If there's one coming soon we should take it. We're wasting time traveling horseback.'

She smiled at him indulgently. He knew then that she had been waiting – without complaint – for him to come to this conclusion. It was his turn to feel embarrassment.

'You could have said something.'

'No. You were looking for your wife. I told you to keep looking. If my husband is dead then there's nothing I can do for him. And in truth I don't know in how much of a hurry I am to see his grave. A few extra days on the trail just didn't seem so important to me.'

They rode on and soon entered the town's main street. The first building they came to stood alone and set off to the side. On its broad adobe front a hand-painted sign read: SVARDT'S GENERAL STORE, and below that in smaller letters: Socorro, New Mexico. Cantrell had never heard of the town.

More buildings began to crowd the street, all of them flat, windswept adobe with small wooden windows and compact hitch rails close to each doorway. There were no raised boardwalks or awnings.

Socorro, it turned out, was a goodsized town, with several streets, and structures that sprawled across the flats toward the foothills of the Magdalenas. It was an active town, too, and the jangling of traces from passing buggies and the murmur of dozens of voices and the scuffling of hurrying feet sounded riotous after a couple of days of relative silence.

A few citizens turned to look at the newcomers, but most ignored them to concentrate on their own business. Keenly, Cantrell scanned the street and the people in it. After a moment he nodded off to their left, toward the train depot. At the railing he dismounted and motioned for Susan to stay with the horses.

'When's the next train north?' he asked the sleepy-eyed clerk nodding off in the ticket-cage. The cage was on the platform side of the depot and Cantrell had to walk around the far end, leaving Susan alone on the street with the horses.

The wiry clerk looked up sharply from beneath his green visor at Cantrell's brusque tone. 'North you say?' He blinked heavily and wiped a knobby hand across his face to rub life back into it. Leaning forward, he consulted a table on the counter, squinting in the growing darkness. After a minute he gave up, got off his stool, and went to light a lamp. 'Been running about three hours behind, lately,' he said, peering at the table again. 'Just had a passenger train come through yesterday. Old number twelve, that damn potboiler.'

An old black man in a striped coat and black cap wrestled a trunk onto a wagonwheel-truck at the end of the platform. A pile of crates was stacked there just outside the freight warehouse section of the depot. A thickset man, alone at the edge of the platform, stared off down the tracks, waiting. He wore a black derby and carried a battered brown carpetbag.

'Where you headed?' the ticket clerk asked.

'Out to Fort Wingate.'

'Wingate's the stop for you, then. But you'll have to switch trains in Albuquerque. Ah, there it is. Ten o'clock tomorrow morning. Six dollars and twenty cents gets you to Albuquerque.'

'I'll get the tickets tomorrow. What about a livery and hotel in town? Any place good.'

'Folks usually ask about food first. I like a man what thinks of his horse. You go to the north end to Whatcom's Barn and Feed. He'll take good care of you. Got one hotel, and it ain't the best, but it's only for one night, right? Silver Shore's it's called. Only building in town that's got a second story to it. Can't miss it.'

Cantrell grinned. 'Thanks. Oh, and what about food?'

'Cantina Felipe. It's across from the hotel. He won't poison you. That's a guarantee. Even wrote it out in Spanish on the wall outside.'

'See you tomorrow,' Cantrell said.

As he turned he noticed the man in the black derby was gone, but his old brown carpetbag sat at the edge of the platform unattended. The porter noticed this, too, and he looked at the bag with deep furrows of curiosity creasing his weathered face. Cantrell didn't pause. That niggling sensation he'd felt on the road was stronger here, compelling him to return to Susan.

He stepped quickly around the corner and ran into the man with the black derby. He had removed his coat to unveil thickly muscled arms that made heavy bulges in his shirt. Cantrell didn't see the man's coat, and too late he saw the hamlike fist shoot up from the stranger's hip. Pain rocketed through Cantrell's head and the world started to buzz and turn white. He felt his knees give out and then he sank into a warm, electric oblivion.

CHAPTER FIVE

Smacking against the rough platform boards jarred Cantrell, shaking the blindness from his eyes. His head slapped against the wood. The buzzing stopped, replaced by pain. Slowly his eyes cleared and as he turned his head he could see a shape silhouetted in the glow of a street-lamp.

Cantrell lay on his back, his entire body still stinging from the blow he'd taken. His focus returning, he could make out the large man in the derby hat rubbing his fist with the palm of his right hand.

'Here now!' the clerk called out impotently, craning against the bars of his cage.

The big man paid him no attention.

Breathless, Cantrell asked, 'What's your beef, mister.' The man had a gun strapped to his hip but it looked like a toy, inconsequential against his bulk. Cantrell tried to shift his weight so he could make a grab for his Colt if needed.

'Name's McIntyre,' the man told him, his voice rumbling almost musically. 'Ain't got no trouble with you, Mr Cantrell. But I aim to kill you.'

McIntyre took a short step forward. Light from the two

platform lamps cast their yellow glow further now that the sun was down. Shadows receded across some of the big man's features, throwing his large grinning mouth and deep-set eyes in stark contrast to the lit portions of his face.

McIntyre's beefy hand stayed clear of his gun, and he seemed unconcerned as Cantrell inched his hand toward his own gun. The man's eyes fairly gleamed with excitement.

'Get up.'

Cantrell, clear-headed now, waved at McIntyre. 'I like it right where I am, friend. I think it's better we talk before things get out of hand.'

The thick-bodied man laughed, throwing his head back carelessly. When he looked back at Cantrell he punched his own hand a few times. McIntyre was no stranger to fist-fighting. He might well have done it professionally, or at least as professionally as things got in the West. Most fist-fighters were exhibitionists; bare-knuckle brawlers who would come into a town and offer to take on any or all of the local toughs. Many wagers were made and, from the looks of the big man, he had come out on the high end of most bets.

Cantrell had done some fighting, too, in the army. He hadn't done badly, but not well enough to take on this man.

McIntyre shook his head. 'This ain't personal, friend. I just gotta tear you up. Now get on your feet or I'll stomp ya where you lay.'

Cantrell nodded, holding up a hand in a weak attempt to keep the giant at bay. Weakly he got to his knees and then forced himself to his feet as if he were pulling himself out of a bog. Cantrell reached back to pull his holster forward. It had twisted about him when he fell. McIntyre flinched, his eyes narrowed just a bit.

'That the way you're gonna do it?' he asked.

'Only way I see I've got a chance,' Cantrell explained.

The big man let out a gusting sigh, supremely disappointed. 'You got less of a chance using iron, friend. That's straight.' To illustrate his sincerity, McIntyre unbuckled his gunbelt and let it slip to the ground.

'You men take this elsewhere!' the clerk squawked.

With his face curled in a sneer, McIntyre lurched forward with surprising speed. He held his arms out as if to scoop up Cantrell but at the last moment shifted his ample heft and swung his right fist in a blinding cross. Cantrell saw this too late. He turned, ducking, but McIntyre's blow caught him high on the left shoulder. Rocked off balance, Cantrell stumbled toward the edge of the platform, tripped then rolled, again ending up on his back.

McIntyre's momentum carried him around and in two thundering steps he stood over his victim.

Not waiting for the big man to make his next move, Cantrell lifted his feet and slammed his spurs down onto the Scotsman's huge thighs. McIntyre howled like a coyote, his knees bent reflexively even as his back arched in agony. Rolling to his feet, Cantrell squared around and, using his full weight and muscle, drove his right fist into the big man's eye.

McIntyre swatted viciously as if slapping at a gnat. His meaty hand caught only air. Cantrell stepped back inside the big man's reach and jabbed a blow at the bloody gash in the Scotsman's left thigh. Blood spurted up through his ruined wool pants. McIntyre let go with another animal scream and dropped to one knee.

'Who sent you?' Cantrell asked, panting for air.

An evil grimace cracked McIntyre's face. 'I do my own fighting, ya desert rat. I saw your kit and your woman and I mean to have them.'

The idea of Susan in this monster's grasp sent a chill through Cantrell. He'd left her alone too long now and the worrisome thought that she'd come looking for him grabbed his gut with an icy grasp. Thinking of her, he didn't see McIntyre's heavy fist rocket toward him. The balled, oak-hard hand slammed the side of his head like a cannon shot cutting through a corsair's hull. Cantrell dropped, barely clinging to consciousness.

Lumbering to his feet, McIntyre groaned and stumbled from the pain of the gouges in his thighs. He took two shaky steps toward Cantrell. He flexed his thick fingers, his heavy chest swelling as he took in a deep draught of air. Cantrell, his head swimming, scrambled to his knees like a drunk looking for the edge of the floor. Weakly, he kicked out with the toe of his boot and caught McIntyre's shin. The big man yelped like a little dog but did not slow his stride.

Rigidly, almost mechanically, he cranked his fist back then swung it in a sideways arc toward Cantrell's head. The fist connected, but only slightly, glancing off Cantrell's temple. It was enough. A burst of colored lights exploded in his eyes as he skittered across the platform, his face scraping against the boards.

Cantrell maintained his senses, just barely. As he slid toward a wrought-iron bench he rolled and clumsily drew his revolver. His hand trembled and the gun seemed to weigh as much as a blacksmith's hammer. He fired a shot at the fuzzy shape stomping toward him. He heard the crack and saw the flash of the shot and then immediately a *thwapping* sound as the bullet struck something. His vision clearing for just a moment, he saw McIntyre grab at his upper arm, a red stain welling between the man's thick fingers.

Growling furiously, McIntyre turned and trudged away as Cantrell loosed a second, wild shot.

The gun was impossible to hold. Cantrell dropped it then clawed his way up the side of the bench and into the seat. Through a hazy view, he looked around for McIntyre but didn't see him. Deep relief that had flooded into him vanished in a wave of cold terror when he heard Susan scream.

An electric shock of energy coursed through Cantrell. He scooped up the Colt, held loosely in his numb fingers, and lurched toward the street.

Susan clung to the black's saddle, kicking wildly at McIntyre's head. His thick, short-fingered right hand had a lock on her left leg, and with his left hand he made stabbing grabs at her shoulder. Susan's writhing made it impossible for him to catch hold of her.

Cantrell raised the gun and aimed, but he couldn't see clearly enough for a good shot. He lowered the gun and fired at the ground. The ricochet snapped like a broken tree limb between McIntyre's feet. The big man jumped with surprise and turned. Just then Susan kicked him squarely in the nose.

McIntyre roared with pain and threw both hands up to his face. Cantrell, at a dead run, plowed into him with his shoulder, knocking the brute off balance and sending them both careening against the black's flanks. The horse screamed with terror and bucked.

'Get out of here!' Cantrell yelled to Susan.

Frantically, she pulled on the reins, but the horse's own wild efforts to get free had tightened the rawhide around the hitching-post. Seeing this, Susan slid out of the saddle and ran for the depot.

McIntyre swatted blindly at Cantrell, clipping his shoulder and shoving him out of the way. The big man stepped clear of the wild, bucking horse, edging further out into the street. Cantrell followed him. His gun was lost and his hand was still stinging. Yet he balled his fist and drove it with all his might into McIntyre's back, just above the kidneys.

Infuriated, McIntyre spun around and swiped viciously at Cantrell. The blow caught him in the chest and sent him stumbling back several paces.

McIntyre grinned madly. His face was bloody, with cuts on his lips and across the bridge of his nose. His left eye was puffy and red. He breathed like a lumbering steam-engine. The madness disappeared for just a moment as fleeting intelligence showed in his eyes. He was hurt and knew it. He might not be able to finish this fight with his fists. But Cantrell was nearly spent, too, and the big man saw this. Slowly, the grin returning to his face, he balled up his massive paw.

Cantrell did not hesitate. He charged forward and slammed into the big man's body with his shoulder. The force of his charge made McIntyre stumble backward just as an ore-wagon trundled around the corner. McIntyre hit the raised side of the bed, his shoulder catching on an exposed nail. With a howl, he swung his fist down across

73

Cantrell's shoulders.

The wagon's driver called out, livid and afraid as his team started into a gallop. In a moment the wagon was gone, leaving behind a swirling mass of dust. McIntyre stumbled into a pair of horses tied to a hitch rail. Rifles were strapped to each saddle. Pawing furiously at one he ripped a rifle from its scabbard. McIntyre spun, blood and dust clouding his eyes, and fired blindly. Down the street a horse cried out in pain as the errant bullet struck. Other animals on the street began to fidget and whinny.

Under cover of the dust, Cantrell charged forward again and sent a smashing right into McIntyre's jaw. The big man faltered, struggling with the gun held loosely in his hands. Cantrell hit him with another right and then a left to his midsection. Stumbling backward, McIntyre bounced against the rear flank of a mule. The animal bucked and shoved the big man away, right into Cantrell's fist.

His round, fleshy face bloodied and puffy, McIntyre raised his hands and pointed at Cantrell's head. It took him a moment to realize the rifle was gone. Wobbling, he bent in search of it in the street. Cantrell was about to step forward and deliver another punch when the mule bucked again. Its left rear hoof caught McIntyre square in the temple sending a gout of blood spurting into the air. The big man collapsed instantly, as if his bones had turned to water.

McIntyre hit the street with a pounding thud and died.

His own body drained of strength, Cantrell collapsed, landing on his backside, his head swimming. A crowd had gathered some time during the fight. He hadn't noticed them, but now they bunched around him and McIntyre's body in curious wonderment.

Susan pushed through the excitedly murmuring crowd. Seeing Cantrell she dropped beside him, taking his face in her hands. Gently, she caressed his temples and smoothed back his hair. He grinned at her lopsidedly, using what little strength remained in him. Her eyes began to glisten.

'Sorry,' he said weakly.

'What for?'

'Shouldn't have brought you in. These towns can get rough.' His tongue had been probing his teeth, feeling for breaks. It felt as if every tooth were loose in his head. Sticking a finger into his mouth he felt along the molars. They were solidly in place, although sensitive to the touch.

'Let's get over to the hotel and get you cleaned up.'

Susan stood and, reaching down with both hands, helped Cantrell to his feet. She had a strong grip. On his feet, he wobbled. She lifted his right arm up and around her shoulders and took his weight on them. A man with a gentle, puffy face stepped forward from the dozens of onlookers and slipped Cantrell's left arm over his shoulders. For an instant, suspicion flared in Susan's eyes and she protectively pulled Cantrell toward her.

'Don't mean no harm, ma'am,' the stranger said.

'Susan,' Cantrell said, 'it's OK.'

She nodded and offered a silent, contrite apology to the stranger.

'Hold up there!'

The crowd parted to let a bowlegged, middle-aged man through. He was a lean fellow, rangy, with tight muscles in his neck and face and along his exposed forearms beneath rolled-up sleeves. He wore a leather vest and a short-crowned hat. Pinned to the vest was a dented, weathered star.

Cantrell relaxed when he saw the star and smiled wanly. 'Do something for you, Marshal?'

The marshal's face soured. 'I'm Henry Killingame, mister, and you guessed rightly. I'm the law around here. You'll need to explain yourself to me.'

'He'll do it from a hotel bed, Marshal,' Susan said. 'Now, if you've a doctor in this barbaric town I would ask you to send him to us immediately.'

She didn't wait for a reply, carefully turning Cantrell toward Silver Shore's wide front porch. The crowd parted again and formed a path up the steps and into the hotel. The clerk, bug-eyed and his face flushed with excitement, was waiting at the front door, solicitously bowing and smiling.

'I'll send the doctor along when he comes,' he promised.

Cantrell signed for two rooms, paid, then took the keys held in the clerk's sweaty palms and started up the broad staircase. The stranger stayed with Cantrell and Susan until they reached the room.

Susan helped ease Cantrell on top of the covers, arranging pillows for him. It was a poor room, as spartan as the army quarters at Fort Craig. Cantrell didn't even bother to look around. Instead he reveled in the simple act of lying down on a soft bed.

'I've known you a week,' Susan said, filling a bowl with water and bringing it to him along with a towel, 'and about all I've done is to take care of your injuries.'

'Guess I'm a bit careless, ma'am.'

'Trouble is more like it.'

She sat on the edge of the bed and began cleaning his face of blood and dirt. Killingame entered the room and leaned up against the doorjamb.

76

'That's what I was thinking, mister. How long you been in town?'

'Maybe an hour.'

'An hour? And a man's dead. I don't think I want you in my town.'

Susan jumped to her feet and turned on the marshal, violently squeezing the wet towel in her fist. 'Tobias did not start the fight! That . . . man . . . attacked me and tried to. . . .'

Cantrell put a hand on her forearm and gently pulled her back onto the bed.

'Marshal, we'll be on the train tomorrow morning. We won't bother you any more.'

A dark-haired man in a frock-coat carrying a black Gladstone bag edged past the lawman and into the room.

'Doc,' Killingame said.

Without preamble, the doctor sat on the opposite side of the bed and began examining Cantrell.

'My name's Polcroft,' the doctor said. 'I'll be charging you two dollars, by the way. Three if you need bandages or medicine.'

'Got my own nurse, Doctor,' Cantrell said, tossing his head toward Susan. 'She can handle these bumps.'

'Bumps, huh?' Polcroft said gruffly.

The doctor lifted Cantrell's shirt, pressed on his abdomen and probed his ribs. The examination lasted less than five minutes. Polcroft stood and went to the wash-basin to rinse his hands.

'He gonna live, Doc?'

'He will. Don't lose that nurse of yours, mister.'

'Better he should avoid fights. At least in my town.'

Polcroft went to retrieve his bag and looked pointedly

at Cantrell. Susan stood up and, with great annoyance, thrust two dollars into the doctor's hand. Tipping his hat, Polcroft turned toward the door.

'Just bumps and bruises, mister. Take it easy for a few days. You'll be fine.'

They watched him go, leaving an awkward silence in the room.

'You want to tell me what happened now?'

Cantrell explained as best he could. There wasn't much he could tell the marshal.

'Didn't know him?'

'Never saw him before. He was on the station platform, waiting for something. He never even looked at me.'

'And he didn't say anything to you?'

'Nothing more than I told you. He wanted Susan and the horses.'

Killingame nodded. 'Them horses. Two of them have army brands. Mind telling me how you came by them?'

'Fort Craig. Lieutenant Garther outfitted us for our trip to Fort Wingate.'

'Because your husband is dead,' he said, glancing at Susan, 'and your wife is missing.'

'That's it.' Cantrell swung his legs off the bed and reached for the towel. Susan snatched it up and wet it, then placed it across the back of his neck. The cool weight of it felt good on his skin.

Footsteps sounded in the hallway and a moment later the porter from the depot edged into view. He carried a beaten brown carpetbag. Killingame waved the man in, and he stepped inside uncertainly.

'That the bag you mentioned?' Killingame asked Cantrell.

'Looks like.'

'What about you?' the marshal asked of the porter. 'You see who belonged to this?'

'Big fella lying dead in the street. He had it. Was at the platform for a couple of hours just waiting.'

'And he started beating on this man here for no reason?'

The porter shook his head. 'Didn't see this fella do nothin' but ask about tickets.'

'Check with the ticket-clerk,' Cantrell suggested. 'He'll tell you the same.'

Killingame grabbed the bag out of the porter's hand, dropped it on the bed and opened it, clearly annoyed. Inside the bag he found a clean shirt, a box of bullets, and a stack of greenbacks banded together with a strip of paper. Killingame examined this closely.

'Five hundred dollars,' he said as he flipped through the bills. 'Lot of money for a man to leave behind in a bag. Any idea why he'd have this much cash?'

Cantrell shrugged. Seeing the money had made him as curious as Killingame. A thought nudged its way out of his subconscious but he didn't give voice to it.

Killingame showed it to the porter who stared greedily at it. 'If I'd known that was in the bag I'd've taken it, that's for sure.' Shaking his head, cursing himself for a fool, the porter left the room.

'This paper band is from the bank here in town. Guess I'll go check it out.' Killingame grabbed the bag and turned toward the door. 'You'll stay put until the train tomorrow?'

'We've got some business to handle and we'll want to eat.'

'Sure,' the marshal said. 'But stay out of the saloons. Come back here right smart, as soon as you're done, or I'll lock you up for the night.'

Not waiting for an answer, Killingame left the room and closed the door behind him.

'I do not like that man,' Susan said stiffly, glaring at the closed the door.

The livery man at Whatcom's Barn and Feed gave a good price for the roan and would have bought the saddle, but Cantrell didn't want to part with it. The army horses he left at the stables, with the livery man promising to return them to Fort Craig.

'I can get me the price of a few days' board to cover my troubles,' Whatcom said, a touch of avarice gleaming in his eyes.

Their arms full of their supplies, Cantrell and Susan went to Cantina Felipe to eat supper. They ate silently.

Several times Susan glanced up at him, the dim candle-light playing shadows across the smooth silk of her skin. She looked exotic in the dim light. He hadn't noticed before that her eyes were shaped more like almonds and dark. A Mexican *señorita*. Like a chameleon, her appearance shifted with the environment. While he recovered from his stabbing she looked pale and soft and sweet. On the road she had taken on a weathered looked beneath a wide-brimmed hat and covered in trail dust. And here in Felipe's she looked like a Mexican maiden, sultry and sweet and a little dangerous.

In silence they returned to their rooms.

'You're bruising badly,' she said, suddenly.

'It looks worse than it is. It felt good to stretch and fill

80

my stomach. Hated to lose the roan, though.'

'I told you I have some money.'

'Save it until we need it. We don't know what we'll find at Fort Wingate.'

They had dumped their belongings in Cantrell's room. She came to him, standing very close, and placed her hand on his arm.

'I-I'm a little afraid,' she confided.

'Why?'

'I guess of what we'll find at the fort.'

His hands were on her arms now, caressing them soothingly. She had changed back into her heavy blue traveling dress after bathing at the barbershop. She smelled fresh and flowery. The scent left him feeling a little light-headed. Susan pressed closer and he found his arms slipping around her waist.

'I almost want to turn back. Maybe the colonel was right. Maybe not knowing is best.'

A deep pang of guilt stabbed at his gut. He hadn't repeated to her what Lieutenant Garther and the corporal had told him that night at Fort Craig. Whether it was true or not didn't matter. The army had dismissed the incident, had buried the truth along with Susan's husband. Susan could only stir up trouble for herself if she knew.

Her breathing became slow and deep as she looked up at him, so close, waiting expectantly. He looked down at her, couldn't look away. He was mesmerized by those almond eyes that still held their exotic appeal. Without thinking he leaned toward her, his hands roughly pulling her up to his mouth, and kissed her. She didn't struggle or pull away. Instead she leaned into him, snaked her arms around his back and clung to him desperately.

Too soon their lips parted. He pushed her away, gently, and walked her to her room across the hall. When she was inside he went back to his room and locked the door. Guilt tore at him mercilessly. At first he had used Susan and her quest to further his own hopeless mission. Then, listening to the furtive corporal whisper in the shadows of Fort Craig, he had wanted to keep Susan away from trouble. Now he knew that he had failed. Someone wanted her dead. Of that he was certain. Someone knew she was heading to Fort Wingate and that she would stir up trouble. And that someone had sent McIntyre to kill her.

The man hadn't given much thought to Cantrell other than that he was someone on which to practice his brutish skills. Cantrell was to be disposed of so McIntyre could murder Susan. McIntyre's boast had been echoing in his mind for hours now and he knew that the man had been lying. The big Scotsman had $500 in new bills, fresh from the bank. He didn't need to steal anyone's supplies. He could have been crazy but Cantrell knew better than that. McIntyre fought like a professional, like a man who hired out his singular skills and coolly enjoyed beating other men.

But he had mentioned Susan. He had known of Susan. Someone had paid him a lot of money to have her killed. Someone who didn't want the truth about her husband's death revealed.

CHAPTER SIX

Sullenly, Cantrell stared out the train window, at the endless low rolling hills and the wide grassy meadows. Little changed in the hours since they boarded.

Seeing that Cantrell was not in a talkative mood, Susan sought out her own thoughts. It surprised her to find little to occupy her time. For days now she had buried her emotions and speculations, intent on the sole mission of proving that her husband was indeed dead. Now, with time on her hands, she realized that she had not only buried her thoughts but also her husband. Very deep.

She felt foolish as her mind drifted back to the kiss she and Cantrell had shared the night before. She wasn't a schoolgirl, she chided herself. A man and a woman kissed for many reasons. That each was lonely and needful of compassion was to be expected. Still, guilt nagged at her. She had never betrayed William, even during his long absences. Yet now, somehow, she felt she had. She had betrayed the ideal that he thought he had married.

Tobias, she realized, had no illusions about a woman. During those few days traveling on horseback he had accepted her as an equal. For the first time in memory she had not been pampered. Even now, she was responsible

83

for carrying half of their belongings, a cumbersome collection of sacks and bags. The thought of that made her smile softly.

William had been an Eastern man, bored with life in the East and desirous of the still-burgeoning adventures in the West. She hadn't understood at the time the allure the wilderness held for him. She thought he would make a fool of himself, but he hadn't. He had excelled and had risen to a position of command. William always had a way about him that could inspire others. Thinking about that now sent a small pang down into her breast. She had stopped loving him, but she could still feel pride for him and what he had accomplished. Had it been selfish of her to dismiss his dreams? Probably, she thought. Looking out on the flowing, seemingly endless landscape rolling by her window she felt the attraction that William must have felt. As she stared out at it she began to drift off.

After some hours Cantrell noticed that Susan had fallen asleep. For long moments he stared at her, entranced by the soft glow that encompassed her face as she slept. He noticed for the first time that, with her expression relaxed, there was a fleshy line along her jaw where her jowls would become prominent. It gave him a glimpse of Susan twenty years in the future as age began to wear on her and he smiled. She would be as beautiful then as she was now.

If he could keep her alive.

The thought sobered him and he again looked about the train car. They were safe for the time, he knew. McIntyre's employers had expected him to succeed. They wouldn't know about the big Scotsman's failure until Cantrell and Susan appeared at the fort.

That morning, Marshal Killingame had met them at the

depot, his dour expression cut only by the relief that Cantrell was leaving town. Killingame had been busy the previous evening and that morning. He'd found out that McIntyre had come to town from the south with a sack of silver and had gone to the assay office. From there he'd taken a receipt to the bank where he received almost $600 in bills. The Scotsman had spent the rest of that day – the day before Cantrell and Susan had arrived – buying new clothes, a box of fat cigars, and drinking. With his old carpetbag in hand he had wandered about the town aimlessly until he eventually went to the train depot. He had stood there patiently until Cantrell had arrived.

'You figure he anticipated me going to the station?' Cantrell had asked.

Nodding, Killingame said, 'Probably saw you ride into town and figured you'd show up there sooner or later to buy tickets. The question is why.'

Killingame was a canny old hand. His suspicions ran deep.

'Thought he was a bounty hunter,' the marshal had said. 'But that didn't make sense, especially him going after the woman. Now you I could see being wanted for something. Maybe something bad.'

Cantrell grinned and rubbed his freshly shaven face. He had lived for months without getting near a razor, but that morning the need for a shave had been strong.

'I've kept to myself, Marshal. No warrants out on me.'

'I know. I checked over every dodger I ever had last night and not a one looked like you. Quite a shame, too. I was kinda looking forward to locking you up. Had a dodger on McIntyre, though. Want to know about him?'

The Scotsman was an itinerant boxer; a man who went

town to town challenging local toughs to bare-knuckle matches and betting on the outcome. He generally did well, and few could match him for sheer strength. But the man was dumb as an ox and lost his winnings in the gambling halls as quickly as he earned them.

'Nothing illegal in that,' Cantrell said.

'Not unless he hires out to kill.'

The wily lawman had hit it on the head, but Cantrell didn't confide in him. McIntyre had been hired to kill Susan. The $500 had been his pay-off. Colonel Jesperson had sent word to Fort Wingate the day Susan had arrived at Fort Craig enquiring about her husband. Within a few days, while Susan nursed Cantrell back to health, the messenger had returned. Cantrell figured that someone at Wingate had heard Susan was investigating and decided to get rid of her, tapping McIntyre for the job. The big Scotsman had made it south to Fort Craig quickly enough but waited until Cantrell and the woman were far enough away from the fort before striking. Or maybe he had missed them at Fort Craig and had had to double back, catching up with them in Socorro.

How he had found them didn't really matter. What concerned Cantrell was who had hired the Scotsman. Was it a soldier? Or someone else? Whoever it had been had a dark secret he was keeping. He wouldn't be happy to see Susan step off the train at Wingate.

They spent the night in Albuquerque, then took another train the next morning which headed west into the mountain regions of the San Mateo range. Skirting around those broken, piñon-studded peaks, the train heaved its iron bulk to a wide mesa littered with sage. Twice they stopped for water and fuel, and they made six stops at small towns. As the sun began setting, Cantrell spied the Zuni Mountains in a lambent haze through the windows on their left. Although distant, the darkly shadowed glow of the setting sun accentuated the reddish tint in the rock.

The trip was not an easy one. The seats were hard and there was little room to move. Standing was difficult because of the sudden and often violent rocking motion of the train. Twice Susan stumbled as she tried to stand and stretch. Cantrell rose the third time with her and wrapped a protective arm around her waist, holding tightly with his free hand to the railing of the luggage-rack above their seats. He didn't look at her as he did this, instead studying very carefully the several gouges in the wood-paneled wall near his bench seat. Two of them looked like marks left by arrowheads. Two others had the distinctive radiating pattern of bullet holes.

He could sense Susan's eyes on him. He expected her to tense because he ignored her. She didn't. Instead, she relaxed, quit fighting the motion of the train, and allowed herself to press up close to Cantrell.

'Thank you,' she said, retaking her seat. 'I've never quite got the handle of riding trains. I came West aboard a boat which landed in Galveston and traveled by stage-coach to New Mexico.'

'Not an easy way to travel,' he said. Sitting again he realized his heart had been thudding as they stood. Although he'd held her for only a few minutes his arm felt empty now.

They debarked with six other passengers onto a wide platform littered with boxes and crates and luggage. Half a dozen uniformed soldiers stood about, smoking, laughing, their rucksacks close to their feet. Mustered out, Cantrell thought. He could see the wide-eyed kinetic energy shimmering off them. They had lived through it and were going home to girls and green grass and soft beds.

The depot was about the only structure in town made completely of wood, a rare commodity so far from the forests of the north. The other buildings, low-lying and thick-walled, were built of adobe and appeared to rise up seamlessly from the desert clay of the same reddish hue. The streets were narrow and already lanternlight from the many buildings spilled out onto the darkening main street.

A porter at the depot told Cantrell where he could find rooms for the night. It was, Cantrell thought, too late to ride out to the fort, only a few miles away. Tomorrow they would rent horses and call on the camp commander. The hotel was several blocks from the depot.

With their satchels and bags and the saddle slung over Cantrell's shoulder, he and Susan looked more like refugees than travelers. They drew attention from a number of people on the street. Wingate rumbled and echoed with the thrum of activity. The day was drifting away and people were eager to finish their business. The casual looks they received were harmless. But after a while Cantrell felt stronger eyes on them. Pausing as if to get his bearings he cast about and found two men standing in the doorway of a saloon. Backlit by gritty lanternlight their features were hard to make out. One of the men wore his hat in a Montana peak and his gun was on the left side. The man next to him was shorter by a few inches and wore a flat-crowned hat. Two guns were strapped rather high on

88

his hips. Each man leaned lazily against the doorjamb, the batwings to their backs. Neither man made any special effort to hide his interest. Still, Cantrell didn't look at them for more than a few seconds before he turned up the street again and continued on to the hotel.

His actions did not pass Susan's notice. She watched Cantrell intently and, when he turned back to her and smiled, she knew that something was wrong. She fought against the urge to look around the street.

After checking in, they went to dinner at a restaurant next to the hotel. They talked generally, and very little at that. Susan could see that something was working on Cantrell's mind so it didn't surprise her when he left her at the hotel, saying he'd be back in an hour.

'Tobias,' she said, laying a hand on his arm. 'Be careful.'

'I'll see you soon.'

The saloon was called the Dog's Leg and the name was painted in thick red letters on the flat face of the building. There were two small windows on either side of the batwing doors, both set high in the wall. Shutters rather than glass covered the windows. Like many of the buildings, a heavy, sturdy wood ladder rested against a side wall for access to some small room on the roof.

The tinny sound of an out-of-tune piano drifted out to the street along with the murmur of men talking low. Lanternlight spilled onto the ground. No one was in the doorway now.

Cantrell left his rifle in the hotel room, taking only the Colt strapped to his hip. He drew the gun, checked the loads, then slid the weapon back into its leather. He didn't know if the men he'd seen earlier that day would be in the saloon, but he felt they would be. They might have been challenging him, standing so boldly and openly watching him. More likely, though, they hadn't known him or Susan by sight but were simply checking out newcomers.

He'd seen the type in dozens of towns. Troublemakers, quick with an insult and even faster with a gun. Instinctively, Cantrell knew that these were men he would have to deal with, and were possibly the ones who had hired McIntyre. The thought sprang to mind the moment he had seen them and it had taken all of his self-control to bury his anger, turn away, and see Susan to safety. Sliding his Colt into its holster, he no longer felt that constraint.

Only one man turned toward him as he entered the saloon. The man was a drunk ranch hand, his eyes bleary, his belly falling over his belt. He wore a stupid grin and his head wobbled on his neck as he turned a blind eye toward Cantrell then back again to the scuffed bar.

Cantrell found a spot at the bar and ordered a beer. The tinny piano changed keys and reached for a Southern reel, but the piano-player's rhythm was off and the sound he made was discordant. Someone threw a beer mug at him, just missing his head to crash against the upraised backboard. Instantly the musician, a wiry, nervous man, switched to a bawdier tune. This he played well enough to keep from being assaulted.

Sipping his beer, Cantrell let his eye roam about the dark, low-ceilinged room. Kerosene lamps bolted to the stone walls cast yellowish pools of light down in tight circles. Between these was a smoky maze of gray in which men sat, played cards, drank, and talked. The tables and chairs were rough-hewn, uneven. Someone had made them by hand without an interest in craftsmanship. The bar was little more than a varnished plank of wood laid across adobe abutments. Behind the bar were two shelves, one for glasses and one for the half-dozen bottles of cloudy liquor. A wooden stand held a beer-barrel. The remnants of some painting were peeling off the wall above the liquor bottles.

Too warm and bitter for his taste, he set aside the beer and turned to face the room. From his pocket he took a bag of tobacco and papers and rolled a cigarette. After a moment he felt eyes on him from across the room. He avoided looking in that direction and took an interest in a card game at a nearby table.

He was almost finished with his cigarette when someone stepped out of the shadows and up to the bar beside him. A smaller man followed discreetly, watching intently.

'Rye,' he called to the bartender and dropped a rattling dollar onto the bar. The bartender brought two glasses and a full bottle and reached for the dollar. His hand stopped just before picking up the coin, reached instead for a towel and began cleaning glasses. Cantrell, intent on the card game, had seen all of it out of the corner of his eye.

'Have a drink, mister,' the man said.

Cantrell lifted his beer glass casually. 'Still working on this,' he said, not taking his eyes from the card game.

This was the taller of the two men, the one who wore a Montana peak and a left-handed gun. His clothes were trail-dirty and his face showed a week's worth of beard, scraggily, untrimmed. Despite his appearance, the man's skin was smooth and pale. He'd done little work out in the sun.

The man tensed at Cantrell's refusal. He poured a second drink none the less and slid it up against Cantrell's elbow.

'Take it,' the man said. He smiled but there was an edge to his voice. 'It's better than that cow-piss you're trying to swallow.'

Cantrell faced the man, his face blank, empty of the enmity he felt. He put down the beer-mug. He took the offered shot-glass and raised it in salute. 'Your health,' he said.

The man chuckled. 'Oh, I'm healthy, mister. I stay real healthy.'

Cantrell drank then reached out to take the bottle. He refilled his host's glass and his own. A violent look came into the man's eyes.

'Got a name?'

Cantrell told him. 'How about you?' The question wasn't casual or friendly.

'Marklin.'

A few others drifted toward them. Cantrell noted Marklin's sidekick, the discreet man who wore a flat-crowned hat.

'Who's that?' Cantrell asked.

Shocked at being singled out, the man darted looks from Cantrell to Marklin.

'Why you want to know?'

Cantrell refilled his glass. Although bitter, the rye was rather weak. 'Saw you two eyeing me earlier on my way into town.'

'His name's Beckert, and we weren't eyeing you.'

The others laughed, including Beckert.

'That woman you were with caught our interest.'

92

Turning to look squarely at Marklin, Cantrell said, 'She's caught mine, too.' His dark tone was unmistakable.

'No offense, friend.'

There were smiles all around, knowing full well that Marklin had meant offense. There was the growing buzz of anticipation in the room. The card-players glanced up warily and after that kept one eye on Marklin.

'You looking for work?'

Cantrell shook his head, his attention again on the card-players.

'Got a job.'

'Around here?' Curiosity darkened Marklin's voice.

'Nope.'

'Then why come to this bit of hell?'

The others laughed and refilled their glasses.

'Why, for the conversation, Marklin. What else?'

They drank for a while. Cantrell rolled another cigarette and paid for another bottle. The others accepted his hospitality warmly, but Marklin and Beckert continued to watch him suspiciously. Cantrell forced himself not to grin at their obvious confusion. He could tell Marklin's first instinct was to beat the information he wanted out of Cantrell, and Beckert would be the first to hold his friend's coat. But Marklin was smart enough to realize Cantrell would not be easy to take down.

'You got work around here?' Cantrell asked.

'For the right man, maybe. If he could take orders and work for wages.'

Cantrell's face soured. 'Wages?'

'Good wages.'

'Hmmph.'

After a bit Marklin asked, 'You thinking about it?'

'Did. For all of two seconds, Marklin. Decided against it.'

Marklin turned away, back to the fresh bottle, and poured another drink, tossing it down in a vicious swallow. With his back to Cantrell he made a sly head move and Beckert nodded.

'You look like you had a rough trip,' Beckert said, stepping closer. A measure of bravado had returned to his long, drawn features and modestly brightened his dull eyes. He was surrounded by comrades. He could risk making an offensive remark.

Cantrell smiled. 'It weren't the trip, boys. It's the landing.'

With each man having four or five shots of rye in him, they laughed easily enough. This made Beckert's face turn red and tighten.

'What I mean—'

'I know what you mean, Beckert.'

The cold steel of Cantrell's voice was unmistakable. Now the card-players abandoned their game and left the table. Two other tables emptied. Yet a man at the back of the crowd hung casually on the bar with his elbow. His appearance was one of cool dispassion. He wore a slightly bemused look on his squared face with his new pinched-front buff hat jauntily tilted back on his head. A patch of red hair curled about his forehead from beneath the hat. He wore punchers' work-clothes, but they hadn't yet been dusted, nor had his hand-tooled boots been scuffed. A gleaming revolver hung lazily on his hip. He didn't look at Cantrell directly, instead watching the other men – Beckert in particular, and Marklin, too – pound their chests at Cantrell.

'I don't want no trouble,' the bartender warbled nervously from behind his bar.

Marklin put a hand to the portly man's face and shoved. 'No trouble, Pete. Now beat it.'

'So-so, how did you come by them bruises?' Beckert said, swallowing down the sudden, fearful realization that he was caught in Cantrell's hot gaze.

Cantrell pushed past the others who had surrounded him to reach the bottle of rye on the bar. As he poured more of the muddy whiskey he stood staring down at Beckert. 'You tell me.'

'I figure it was that you had a smart mouth. Maybe somebody decided to shut it for you.'

'He did a poor job of it, then.'

'Seems to me,' Beckert said, his voice beginning to tremble, 'that maybe you need a little more of what you got.'

Cantrell tipped his hat back on his head. 'You going to give it to me?'

'I might.'

'The last guy didn't do so well,' Cantrell said with a grin.

'Looks like he did just fine.'

'He did all right, until he died.'

Beckert shook visibly now and had grayed a little around the gills. Marklin spun and shoved Beckert away. His eyes were hot. Cantrell saw his hand twitching toward his gun. Others saw it, too, and faded into the gray shadows. Cantrell knew for certain then that these two were the ones who had sent McIntyre after Susan.

'You're lying.'

Cantrell shrugged. 'Maybe. You can ask him. Big fellow named McIntyre. Wears a derby. Of course, he wasn't in a talkative mood when I left him.'

'Never heard of the man.' Marklin spoke in a wooden tone.

'Well, if you hurry, you might be able to meet him. He may still be lying in the street with his head stove in and his brains spread out in the dirt.'

Without a word, Cantrell backed away from the crowd toward the door. Marklin stared hotly after him but kept his hands resting on the bar.

'Thanks for the drinks, boys,' Cantrell called, and then was gone.

Beckert's courage screwed tight now, he reached for his gun, his hand trembling. Marklin grabbed his arm and shook his head. With a quick glance he looked back along the bar. The man with the easy smile and new clothes was gone.

Uncertain, Marklin scanned the bar for the other man and, not finding him, released Beckert's arm. Together, the two left the Dog's Leg. On the boardwalk, they moved out of the square of yellow light cast by the meager saloon-lamps and stepped into the shadows.

Ahead Cantrell walked slowly, confidently. He kept his back to the saloon as he sauntered toward the hotel. Shadows swallowed and released him as he walked away, each time his dim shape growing smaller. Again Beckert reached for his gun but was stopped by Marklin.

'He killed McIntyre,' the smaller man protested.

'Maybe.' Marklin didn't sound doubtful. 'And if he did, it's McIntyre's fault. He was sure big enough to do what he should have done.'

'Well, he ain't done it, and now he's dead!'

'Enough, Mr Beckert.'

Startled, the two men spun around at the sound of the

new voice. The red-haired man from the saloon had come up behind them on cat's feet, dark and shadowed by the night. Despite his quietly stern voice Marklin sensed the man was still smiling. He did not look at them, but stared down the street at the disappearing figure of Cantrell.

'Mr Jovane,' Marklin said with deference. 'Did you hear what he said about McIntyre?'

Alec Jovane only nodded. 'He's going back to the woman now. Tomorrow he'll go to the fort.'

'We'll set up on the road,' Marklin offered. 'At Kipper's Point, top of the rock. We'll take care of them both.'

Jovane chuckled lightly. 'No. Let them go.'

Beckert jumped as if bit by a snake. 'But, Jovane! You can't let 'em.'

Hardly had the words left Beckert's mouth when the back of Jovane's hand struck with a clap. Instantly, blood welled up on Beckert's lower lip. Jovane slowly lowered his hand.

'I want to see what this man Cantrell does.' Jovane spoke quietly, standing in the middle of the empty street. 'I want to know who he is, why he's here. He's no lawman, so why does he bother with this business that's none of his concern.'

Carefully, Marklin ventured: 'The woman.'

Jovane nodded. 'Yes. I suppose the woman might be the cause. She is handsome.' His eyes never left the hotel at the end of the street. Cantrell was gone now, inside to the warm glow of the lobby. 'He'll see to her safety. He'll get rid of her for us.'

'And if not?'

Shrugging, Jovane turned and walked away, pale window-light catching a dull gleam in his eye and the stunning whiteness of his smile.

CHAPTER SEVEN

Cantrell walked slowly back to the hotel, keeping to the shadows and watching his backtrail. He had seen some men enter the street, but they didn't seem interested in following him or causing trouble. There might have been an exit in the back of the Dog's Leg so he watched at every corner and alley for an attack. None came. Marklin was smart enough to not make a rash decision. He didn't know enough about Cantrell or why he was here to murder him despite his obvious desire to do so. Yet Cantrell sensed that Marklin had not been the man in charge of the bit of play-acting that had just concluded. The other man, the lazy one at the end of the bar, the one who smiled too easily. That was the boss, Cantrell thought.

But the boss of what? What was it that made these hard-bitten men afraid of a woman? She was the widow of an Army lieutenant, and the corporal back at Fort Craig had intimated that her husband, William Covington, had been murdered. Perhaps Cantrell had read too much into that midnight meeting. Perhaps the corporal, and Lieutenant Garther, had simply been concerned with Susan's well being. Army life was a hard one, especially so for women who didn't or wouldn't understand it. Covington's death was no doubt a gruesome one, with the Apaches involved. There were things about it that she was better off not knowing.

Marklin had been truthful about one thing. He had been watching Susan. He knew her by sight. He might have sized up Cantrell in passing, but his attention had been on the woman and not for the obvious reasons. She meant something to him. Danger, most likely. Her being here would stir things up. What those things were, Cantrell couldn't guess. But he knew that Marklin would kill Susan, given the chance, perhaps as he'd killed her husband.

He paused outside her room for a moment, uncertain whether he should wake her. He was about to turn away when a floorboard creaked and her door swept open.

'Tobias?' she said. She was wearing that nightgown he had seen her in back at Fort Craig. He almost laughed seeing the McWorter lying on the bed behind her.

'Didn't want to wake you.'

'Come in.'

She didn't wait for an answer, pulling at his arm until he was inside. Quickly she shut the door. She had a lamp burning brightly. Cantrell went to it and turned it low so there was barely enough light to see.

'Tobias, what are you doing?'

'Just being careful.'

She looked at him curiously, not fully understanding. He hadn't told her about the clandestine meeting at Fort Craig. He had felt that this trip on which she insisted was a fool's errand, meant to assuage her vanity and guilt. After a few days with her he knew that he'd been wrong about her. While he had used the opportunity for his own futile ends, none of that now seemed very important. Something about the death of William Covington gnawed at Cantrell and because of it he needed to help Susan – if not uncover her husband's killer then to find peace.

'You've been drinking,' she said, a touch of disappointment in her voice.

'A little. I needed to get some answers.'

She nodded. 'You found something about your wife?'

'No. I . . .' The right words wouldn't come into his head. In frustration he went to the window and drew the curtains. She'd be safer in case Marklin decided to take a pot shot from the street. 'Do you really need to see this through?' he asked at last.

Susan came to him, pressing close, her hands clinging to his shoulders.

'I just need to see his grave, Tobias. That's all. Nothing else. He was my husband and I have to say goodbye.'

Cantrell's stomach churned with guilt at keeping from her his thoughts about William's death.

She smiled up at him, holding him close, probing his thoughts with her eyes. Such beautiful hazel eyes lit with a sprinkling of silver dust. She smelled of powder and her own natural musk. He felt her lean body press up against him, her face toward his, caressing his lips with hers, pulling him down to her. Her arms were soft yet powerful, fueled by desire.

This time he didn't push her away.

Cantrell rented two horses the following morning, borrowing a saddle for Susan. It was early when he brought the animals back to the hotel and looped the reins around the hitching post. Few people were on the street. A woman tossed a soapy bucket of water into the thirsty ground. The dry-goods shopkeeper raised a green canvas awning over his door and front window. A tired-looking teamster worked an exhausted mule-team toward a warehouse a block from the railroad depot.

In the doorway to the Dog's Leg Beckert stood with a beer in his hand. He stood in the shadows, behind the batwings, a bleary-eyed, glaring Cheshire cat. The fat saloonkeeper had opened the main doors and was uneasily brooming the boardwalk. He caught sight of Cantrell and jerked to a halt. After a quick glance at Beckert he discarded the broom and hurried into the cavernous shadows of the saloon.

Ignoring the small man, Cantrell went into the hotel, returning a few minutes later with what they'd need for their ride to Fort Wingate. Susan came down moments later, dressed in corduroy pants and yellow blouse and a lined canvas jacket. She did not look like a man, not even with that worn, floppy hat on her head.

Cantrell kept his eye on Beckert, who had not moved since being spotted. With Susan mounted, he climbed atop a rusty gelding and, using his back to shield her, headed them out of town.

The clerk had given them directions to the fort, but the road, wide and well-trod, was impossible to miss. They rode for an hour at an easy pace before Cantrell slowed them, then halted.

'What is it?'

Cantrell shrugged noncommittally. Up ahead there was a bend in the road. At the elbow was a large boulder, big as a house, which rose up at a sharp angle and then appeared to slope away. There didn't seem to be any movement atop the rock.

He started them forward again, around the bend slowly, and then got the horses into a lope to get them away from the obvious ambush point. Glancing over at him, Susan wondered if Cantrell were disappointed. He had looked so ready to fight. Not tense or angry, but determined and loose, as if he would welcome whatever danger that rock represented to him.

In truth, Cantrell was disappointed. He had expected an ambush from Marklin and Beckert, and when it didn't come it left him confused. Why try to murder Susan from far away, but ignore her when she was within their grasp?

Before noon the outpost came into view. Like Fort Craig it was a sprawling mass of buildings and manicured grounds. A backdrop of sharp, red buttes provided relief against the weather-whitened barracks and other structures. Beyond the buttes was the higher, rocky north slope of the Zuni mountain range, spotted with piñon and juniper and cut by trickling streams. There was a lot of activity in camp. Several mounted units loped away from the fort in different directions, flags snapping and bugles braying.

There were more Indians here, all of them being herded with dragging steps toward a roped-off corral. Among their numbers were more men, braves who looked dejected and tired. They walked at a stately pace on leaden feet. Several children, though, unaware of their humiliation, ran in circles and whooped playfully, racing out to tag soldiers with a slap on their arms or chests. The soldiers did nothing to stop the children.

Several covered wagons lined one of the camp's streets, oxen and mule and horses waiting patiently in their yokes.

Impatient were their human masters, pacing along side the wagons and venting anger at whatever hapless soldier passed too closely. Riding past, Cantrell made out some of their complaint. These were dispossessed settlers anxious to return to their land now that the Indian problem was under control.

Near the center of the camp were a dozen men and women, all garbed similarly in duck pants and loose shirts with pocketed belts wrapped around their waists. Some wore pith helmets and others Western hats. They stared at the ground, crouched low, digging into the hard dirt. A table had been set up beneath an open-sided tent and was crowded with shards of pottery and bones and beads. Several of the men were quite excited over a colorfully painted pot just excavated, still whole and apparently important.

Susan watched them, fascinated and confused. She turned questioningly to Cantrell.

'Some sort of scientists,' he said. 'Anthropologists, they call themselves. I've seen them about New Mexico and Texas and Arizona. They're studying the Indians, now that they're being forced off the land. Pots and bones get them real excited.'

'You seem to disdain them. I would have thought with your wife having been kidnapped by Indians you wouldn't care what happens to them.'

'I have no love for the Apache, that's true. Few do. But the Indians are more than the Apache. They're a hundred cultures and more. A thousand. Each one different. Some good, some bad. Some tribes we whites could have lived with, or rather they could have lived with us, if we'd have given them half the chance.'

Susan nodded her understanding. 'They were peaceful

until we came along.'

'That's a fallacy,' Cantrell said. 'Like any culture, some Indians went to war for land or food, making war on other Indians. Whole tribes had been wiped out long before white men came. Other tribes simply wanted to stay on the land of their ancestors and live the only life they've ever known. The Apache, well, they ruined it for all of them.'

'I don't believe that,' she responded confidently. 'Even if all of the tribes had been peaceful, their time running free in the West was over the moment white men came here.'

Cantrell shrugged. 'Maybe.'

A soldier directed them to the camp commandant's office, a utilitarian white house among a row of similar white houses. Two guards stood outside a white picket-fence. They snapped to attention as Cantrell helped Susan dismounted. The rougher-looking of the two guards nodded curtly when Cantrell had explained his mission, then opened the gate to admit the visitors.

Opening the front door they found two large rooms, one off to each side, filled with desks and soldiers uncomfortably seated, shuffling paper. Several of the men had writing-stands and were copying papers. A corporal stood and bowed curtly. He listened to Cantrell's story and then excused himself. Several minutes later they were shown into an office at the back of the house, and the door shut behind them.

'Mrs Covington,' a robust man of fifty-plus years said, rising from behind his desk. 'I'm Colonel Eaton, commander of Fort Wingate.' He wore a sharply creased uniform with colonel's insignia. His voice was warm and friendly with an undertone of sharpness. He took Susan's hand

and shook it, then guided her to a seat. Then he turned to Cantrell.

'I expected Mrs Covington, sir. I didn't know she had a companion.'

'A guide, Colonel,' Susan said, quickly. 'Mr Cantrell has business of his own.'

Hearing Susan call him by his surname felt strange. She had called him Tobias for days now, though it seemed longer than that. He felt as if they'd known each other for years. And after their kiss and embrace last night he thought . . . well, he didn't know what to think. She spoke coolly, as if the intimacy that had developed between them the past week had meant nothing.

'So I understand. I wish I had better news for both of you.'

'Any news would be appreciated, Colonel.'

The door opened and the corporal entered carrying a small pasteboard box, its top open and its lid held underneath the box. He set it on the colonel's desk, saluted, smartly turned, and left. Seeing the small, plain container, Susan shivered.

'I've sent for Captain MacArthur of K Company, your husband's commanding officer.'

As if in a trance Susan leaned forward and began fingering the contents of the box. A uniform, a flag, some ribbons, a wallet, a locket. She opened this and smiled wanly, then snapped it shut. There were two letters at the bottom of the box, both from her, and a third in Covington's hand that had not been finished. Disappointment washed over her face as she pushed the box away and slumped back in the chair.

A knock at the office door startled all of them. A second

105

later another officer entered, this one in captain's stripes. Eaton introduced the newcomer.

'I thought it best if Captain MacArthur were here to answer your questions.'

'My husband is dead, then, gentlemen?'

'Yes ma'am,' MacArthur said. He was a tall and grim-faced with dark hair graying at the temples.

'How did he die?'

'Bravely, ma'am. He and another soldier, Private Stovall, held off an Apache raiding-party that had ambushed them to give the rest of the patrol time to escape with the wounded. A relief patrol arrived too late.'

Susan lowered her head and took a long, slow breath. 'I see. Was he buried with honors, Captain?'

The two officers shared a look of discomfort. 'Mrs Covington, out here on the frontier we don't have the facilities for a ceremonial burial. That we got your husband's remains back was a stroke of fortune. We weren't so lucky with Private Stovall.'

'When did this happen?'

'Three weeks ago, ma'am.'

'Mrs Covington,' Eaton said, 'your husband was an excellent officer. Respected by his men and well liked by this superiors. He served the army and his country well.'

'I see.' Her chin began to tremble. She started to glance up toward Cantrell, then stopped, not wanting to make eye contact. Slowly, she stood. 'I came to see my husband's grave, gentlemen. After that I won't bother you any more.'

'We have a graveyard just outside the camp. I can have an orderly take you.'

'Mr Cantrell will escort me.'

Susan turned and somewhat shakily walked toward the

door. MacArthur snatched up the box on the desk and followed her.

'Mrs Covington,' he said, offering the box. 'You'll want your husband's things.'

'That, sir, is where you are wrong.'

They watched her leave and for a moment none of them said anything. Then Cantrell took the box from the captain. 'She'll want it. After a time.'

Colonel Eaton went to his desk and retrieved an item from the top drawer. He handed it to Cantrell. It was a cameo, onyx on ivory rimmed by silver. The silver was tarnished now, having an almost coppery sheen. Cantrell recognized it immediately and nearly dropped the box.

'I'm sorry, Mr Cantrell. I can see that you know that piece of jewelry.'

'It was my wife's.'

Eaton nodded. 'I suspected so when my corporal informed me of your arrival. She's buried next to Lieutenant Covington. The grave is unmarked. We'll see to a marker if you'll tell me her name.'

'Mary.' He couldn't take his eyes off the cameo. Nearly two years of hoping and anger and frustration were suddenly gone, and he was left with only a numb feeling. 'How did she die?'

Captain MacArthur spoke up. 'She was found south of here. Apparently she had made her escape and had suffered the pains of crossing rough country. The Apaches caught up with her and stabbed her, leaving her to die. A patrol found her but it was too late. She lived for only a little while and never made it back to the fort.'

'I'd like to talk to the soldier who found her.'

MacArthur stiffened with discomfort. 'I'm sorry, Mr

Cantrell. That's impossible. He's dead.'

'What happened?'

'He died fighting Apaches three days later.'

Something in the captain's voice brought Cantrell's attention into sharp focus.

'Who was he? What was his name?'

'Lieutenant William Covington.'

For a moment the words hung in the air, trembling as if caught in a soft breeze. At any moment they would fall and shatter. None of the men spoke or even looked at one another. Cantrell shivered but he didn't feel cold. He felt his face harden with hatred. Even numb, his mind understood, deep down, that MacArthur had left something unsaid.

'Mrs Covington,' Eaton said, 'plans to leave after she has seen her husband's grave. Is that your intention as well?'

Cantrell glanced up sharply at the colonel, his jaw clenched grimly.

MacArthur stepped forward, very close to Cantrell. 'We have investigated, Mr Cantrell. The coincidence is ... pronounced, but not unusual. No one is hiding anything foul. That is, no more foul than these two unnecessary deaths.'

Though severe, MacArthur projected empathy and reason. Cantrell hated him for it, but knew the man was being genuine. He could see the loss in MacArthur's eyes. Somewhere in his long career he had lost someone very dear to him.

Without speaking, Cantrell left the room.

They had left their horses behind at the colonel's house

along with William Covington's possessions. They hadn't spoken since Cantrell told Susan of the strange coincidence of their spouses' meeting. Leaving the fort's confines they walked along a rutted road to the top of a shallow red butte. Piñon grew in abundance atop the butte, along with tufts of thick grass and yellow wildflowers. The sky was cloudless, a deep shade of blue. The cemetery stood at the far end of the butte, surrounded by a neat white fence.

It took but a few moments to locate the two graves. A simple smooth stone marked Mary's grave. A flat stone engraved with Covington's name, rank, and date of death lay at the head of his grave. Atop the stone was a fresh bouquet of colorful wildflowers tied at the stems with a bit of blue lace hair-ribbon.

Susan stared down at the grave, stiff and pale. A single tear slid down her cheek. Cantrell didn't know what to say to her. His heart felt heavy in his chest. She had seen the flowers and, like him, had probably seen the small boot-print in the soft, turned earth beside the grave. A woman's boot-print.

'He had been out here a long time,' she said at last, her eyes welling with tears. After a moment she turned and left the cemetery.

CHAPTER EIGHT

Susan Covington stood on the railway platform, her small bag at her feet, a green bonnet on her auburn hair and white gloves on her tightly clenched hands. William Covington had some back pay due him, and officers and enlisted men alike had taken a collection for the widow, not knowing that finances were the least of her concerns. Colonel Eaton had presented her with the offering and after a moment of hesitation she accepted. With it she had bought a new dress and personal items and a small bag. The floppy hat and the men's clothes were in the bag and would no doubt cause a stir upon her return to Virginia.

She had refused to sit on the bench even though the train was not due for hours. 'If I sit,' she told Cantrell, 'I'll never be able to get up again.'

He stayed with her, after returning the horses and checking out of the hotel. For the longest time he thought she was staring blindly out on the prairie. Drawn to her eyes he saw that they were wide and attentive. A hawk wheeled above then dove for a sparrow. She followed the attack. Children played in the dirt beyond the railroad tracks. She watched every one of their movements. Far off, a cavvy of wild Indian ponies galloped by. She seemed to swell, thrilled with their distant rumble.

Susan was saying goodbye, drinking in as much of the Western horizon as she could, before returning to the confines of her life.

When the train whistle distantly cut the air, Cantrell stepped up to join her.

'It's really quite beautiful,' she said. 'I understand this much about William, at least.'

Cantrell lifted the box he had taken from Eaton's office and held it out for her.

'I can't, Tobias.'

'He gave his life for this land you find so captivating. It's men like him who make it possible for others to follow and prosper. You need to keep that part of him alive, at least.'

'You're a man like that, too, Tobias.' Her voice was soft and her dark eyes were misty. She looked away suddenly. 'I'm not comfortable talking about him to you. Do you understand?'

'No.'

'It's the way I feel about you, Tobias. The way I no longer felt about William.' She leaned close and kissed him lightly on the lips. 'It's not guilt,' she said, pushing herself away from him. 'I don't want to hurt you by talking about him. And I suppose I don't want you to hurt me.'

'I wouldn't do that.'

She smiled sadly. 'You've searched two years for your wife. The night before you discovered her fate you spent it with me.'

There had been, he admitted, a sharp pang of guilt when he had looked down at that unmarked grave. When the army stonecutter chiseled Mary's name into the stone the next morning a sense of release overwhelmed him. He no longer had to fear for Mary. He knew she was in a better place. And knowing that he also knew she would forgive him his seeking comfort in Susan's arms.

He shook his head. 'I'm not sorry for that, and I think she would understand.'

'You suppose we'd like each other?'

'Not under the present circumstances.'

She laughed lightly, bumping against the box he still held out to her. She drew a long slow breath and took the box.

'I suppose I'll thank you for this one day.'

'You will.'

The train pulled up to the platform slowly, wheezing and puffing as it squealed to a stop. The conductor got off and helped passengers debark. Men, mostly. Cow-hands and soldiers and a few businessmen. Two women got off, over-dressed in wide skirts and fighting with parasols, and immediately were swarmed by soldiers waiting on the platform.

'You won't come?' Susan asked, a little too loudly. He shook his head. 'What will you do?'

'I guess do what I've been doing.'

He hadn't expected her to enquire about his plans. He did a poor job of lying to Susan. He had worked out the plan in his head the previous night. William Covington had been murdered, of that he was certain, and not by Indians. His death so close in time to Mary's made him suspicious, too. When he took into account the attack by the hulking brute, McIntyre, he knew that Mary and Covington had stumbled into something that had gotten them murdered. He wanted Susan out of harm's way and the freedom to uncover the truth.

He picked up her bag and walked her to the train. She stopped before getting on.

'You don't owe me anything, Tobias.' She spoke softly, making him strain to hear her. 'We helped each other through a difficult time. But I know that something is bothering you.'

He wanted to smile at her in wonderment. How had she gotten to know him so well in so little time?

'Go home, Susan,' he told her. 'Be happy.'

Without another word or a backward glance he turned and left the platform. The engine, steaming out loud hisses, kept him from hearing her follow after him, down the steps to the street. He had walked nearly a block before sensing her.

'Go back to the train, Susan.' His voice was cold and his eyes were dead. Seeing him that way frightened her.

'No. Something's wrong, Tobias. Something you're not telling me.'

He could feel curious eyes on them as others passed by on their way through town. The urge to look down at the Dog's Leg was strong, but he fought against it.

'I can't go home with doubts about William's death. Not your doubts, Tobias,' she said quickly, seeing him about to protest. 'My own. The colonel and Captain MacArthur were altogether too happy to see us leave.'

'You'll be a tough one to get rid of,' he said, a wry grin cracking his face.

'Do you want to get rid of me, Tobias?'

He didn't answer. Taking her bag and box into his arms he said, 'Come on.'

They checked back into the hotel, then went to the livery stable in the next street and hired horses again. This

113

time he took the extra rifle Lieutenant Garther had given them and slid it into the boot of Susan's rented saddle. He took their travel kits — food, canteens, blankets, and ammunition – and strapped them behind their saddles.

Their preparations were observed rather clumsily by Beckert, the small edgy man from the Dog's Leg who wore a flat-crowned hat pushed back on his head. Another set of eyes watched them, too. Cantrell felt them but couldn't spot them. Eventually, he guessed that the spy was watching from behind a curtain in a second-floor room of the hotel. It didn't matter any more. They hadn't got on the train and these men, whoever they were, would not like it.

Something dark clouded Cantrell's mind. He would be glad to have something to fight. Nothing was in the open. He only had suspicions. But it would all come to the surface soon enough. Beckert was too nervous. He'd make a mistake. Then the others would be forced into showing their hands. Cantrell didn't know what it was all about and he didn't care. At least he would avenge William Covington's death. He would do that for Susan, and a little bit for himself, too.

They rode a ways out of town, Cantrell letting the quiet of the empty plains wrap around them, before he spoke. Then he told Susan what he knew, what he suspected, what Garther and the corporal had tried not to say that night back at Fort Craig.

'Who would murder William?' Susan said, after a few minutes. 'Everyone liked him. Are Colonel Eaton and Captain MacArthur lying?'

'I don't think so. But they've got their reports and if everyone is sticking to the story then there's no cause to question it further. They've lost plenty of men to Indian attacks. It's not a strange story. But I want to look deeper.'

'Oh, Tobias, what do you hope to find?'

'I want to see where Mary was found and where William died. I want to talk to anyone who was there.'

She tried to hide her pity for him, while feeling foolish herself. She had followed him blindly, expecting that he knew something important. But he had nothing, only suspicions, and had given up one obsession for another. Suddenly she was afraid for him. She nudged her borrowed sorrel closer to him as if her proximity might bring him peace.

Beckert ducked back into the Dog's Leg and went to the bar and his waiting bottle of rye. Not bothering with the shot-glass he tilted the bottle to his lips and drank deeply. He was shaking. That damned stranger made him shake. He slammed the bottle onto the bar, alerting others to his mood. There were only a few men in the saloon at that hour: an old alkie, too snookered to lift his head, a couple of grizzled, bow-legged old-timers who'd lived past their usefulness as drovers, and the paunchy bartender. Of that group, only the bartender quailed. The old-timers, playing poker for matchsticks, ignored him as they would a petulant child.

The woman, he wondered with a moment of unnatural clarity. This stranger, was he here about the woman?

Beckert had noticed that the soldier's widow and the stranger seemed close. Her hand touching his lightly. The looks they'd share. Affection, not lust. Well, not entirely affection. Not a widow more than a month and already she had someone to fill soldier-boy's shoes. Well, why not? Soldier-boy had stepped out a time or two himself. The perfect officer, Beckert thought derisively. The men and officers alike thought well of him. But he was like any man stuck out in this wilderness. Lonely, needful of a woman's touch. Beckert had seen soldier-boy and that hat-shop girl together, many times. Molly something or other. No, he was nothing special.

And the widow seemed to be cut of the same cloth. So why hadn't she boarded that train? She had planned to go until the stranger turned away. Now they were heading out to the fort again.

Beckert looked down to see that he had drained his bottle. Wiping a grimy sleeve across his sparsely bearded face he called for another, then told the bartender to forget it.

He felt a little uneasy on his feet all of a sudden. He straightened his gun-belts, then lifted each revolver and checked the loads. The old-timers stopped their play to watch him. Like watching a kid with matches.

Without a word he stepped out of the saloon and into the street. A rider stopped short so as not to run into Beckert. Across the street and down a few blocks was the Star Hotel. Beckert entered the spacious front room and, ignoring the desk clerk, mounted the stairs to the right.

On the second floor he thudded down the hall to a closed door. He heard voices speaking softly, the words indistinguishable. Beckert was about to reach for the knob when he stopped short, his hand shaking again. He removed his hat and quickly ran fingers as a makeshift comb through his hair. He dusted his hat, replaced it carefully, and wiped his boots with the back of his pant legs.

Gently, he knocked.

When the door opened Marklin stood filling the frame,

grinning knowingly at him.

'Come on in, Beckert.'

Now more nervous than he had been before downing a bottle of whiskey, Beckert swept the hat from his head and stepped inside the room just far enough for Marklin to close the door.

The room was as close to a suite as the Star Hotel could manage. There were two rooms, neither of them very big. They were in the main room and the other was through an open doorway lined with a heavy red drape that was pulled back with thick red ties. There were two chairs and a *chaise-longue*, a couple of small tables, and a sideboard with glasses and bottles of liquor. The room was rather blandly decorated and furnished, and none of that mattered to Beckert.

Since entering the room his eyes had locked on Alec Jovane sipping coffee from a china cup at the sideboard. The man was smugly amused.

'Have we gotten an early start, Mr Beckert, or have your night-time activities carried into morning?'

'I been watching that stranger. The one with Covington's widow.'

Jovane let the statement hang in the air for a moment, enjoying the uncertainty that wriggled across Beckert's face.

'And your conclusions?'

Marklin returned to the sideboard and poured a cup of coffee, which he brought to Beckert.

'Drink this,' he said.

'Don't want it.'

'Drink it.'

Marklin didn't look as amused as Jovane. Beckert took

the cup and drained it.

'Followed them down to the train-station, early.'

Jovane grinned. 'Industrious of you.'

'The stranger didn't get on with the widow. He stayed in town. Checked back into the hotel, as a matter of fact.'

'I didn't expect him to leave, Mr Beckert.'

'But the woman didn't go, either. She stayed with him. Changed her mind, is what it looked like.'

Jovane nodded. 'I saw.'

'We gotta do something.'

Arching an eyebrow, Jovane asked, 'Do what?'

'I don't know,' Beckert growled, frustrated. 'I think we oughta gun him down.'

'For keeping company with a widow?' Jovane stood and poured himself more coffee from a silver pot.

'They're going back to the fort. They'll be asking questions.'

'Let them. There's nothing for them to find. Killing them only calls attention to something that doesn't warrant it.' Jovane sipped at his cup, then, putting it down with exaggerated gentleness, he walked the few steps to Beckert. 'Don't make the same mistake you made with McIntyre. That bit of foolishness will not be tolerated again. Do I make myself clear?'

Beckert nodded stupidly, his eyes wide.

'Let those two tire themselves out. They'll be gone soon enough, and we'll keep getting richer.' Jovane reached down and took Beckert's sweat-stained, dusty hat and turned it upside down. Into the cavity he dropped several large coins. Giving the hat back he said, 'Get more coffee for yourself and breakfast. Clean up a bit. Then go out to Piñon Creek and make sure the boys are handling the branding. You've been away too long. We do have other businesses, Mr Beckert.'

'Yes, sir.'

Out in the hallway again Beckert paused, listening. The soft talk resumed, but no laughter. He didn't care how big a man Jovane was, he wouldn't stand for being laughed at.

It took little time for Beckert to realize that Jovane was sending him out of the way. Piñon Creek was in the opposite direction from the way the stranger had gone. Far away from the Zuni Mountains. He began shaking again. That damned Covington. If he had just left well enough alone. It was only some no-good squaw, didn't matter to no one. Unless she'd mattered to the stranger. And if she did matter to him, he wasn't the type to let go and allow the dead to stay dead. Hate welled up in Beckert for the stranger and slowly his shaking hands calmed.

By the end of breakfast Beckert knew what he had to do. He saddled his horse, flipping the stable-boy a quarter.

'I'll be gone a few days.'

The boy didn't care.

Beckert rode out of town to the north-east, toward Piñon Creek, and stayed on the trail for half an hour knowing that his passing stirred up a plume of dust. When he reached Oatil Creek, hardly more than a trickle of water partly shaded by a collar of pale grass, he guided his horse into the water and turned upstream. Oatil Creek would take him north-west far enough to get behind Red Butte and well out of view of anyone watching him leave town – like Jovane's lapdog, Marklin. From there he would circle west and south to the Zuni range. The stranger would go up into the Zunis, eventually, Beckert reasoned. He'd go looking for where that woman was killed but

119

would find Beckert waiting for him with plenty of hot lead.

Lieutenant Griffin looked up sternly past the kerosene lamp, lifted hands coated in blood up to his elbows, and said, 'Can we do this another time? I'd like to save this boy's leg.'

Cantrell glanced down at the young soldier on the table, half his uniform cut from his stiff body. The smell of ether was thick in the close room. Ether and blood and excrement. Susan had insisted on entering the room and though white as a sheet had rolled up her sleeves to help the doctor. She was bathing the wound, washing away the unstanched flow of blood.

'You've bigger problems than that leg,' Cantrell said quietly.

The soldier's head had been crushed under the hoofs of runaway horses. Hardly more than a boy, he'd been caught in the stampede. He wouldn't recover no matter how skillfully Lieutenant Griffin, MD applied his arts.

Griffin paused, furious, to look down at the soldier. The boy, even in an ether-induced coma, began to seizure. With slippery hands, Griffin pinned the soldier by his arms, holding him to the table until he stopped shaking. After a minute or two Griffin straightened, took a towel from the instrument table, and draped it over the young man's face.

For a long time Griffin said nothing, his lined face as gray as his close-cropped hair. He washed his hands then ripped off his bloodied apron and tossed it into a basket in a corner of the room. Ignoring Cantrel, he went through a door into a tiny office and sat at a desk overflowing with papers. He made notes on a pad, then he tossed it aside and took a bottle of whiskey from a desk drawer and poured three fingers of the stuff into a glass. This he downed quickly, then poured some more.

Cantrell stood in the doorway, waiting. Susan finished washing and joined them.

'In the line of duty,' Griffin said. He nodded toward the pad on which he had made his notes. 'That's what the report will read. His parents will get a flag and a uniform we'll dirty up and a story about fighting Indians that the colonel will fabricate. With luck they'll never know what a damn fool that kid was.'

Griffin finished his second glass of whiskey and sourly contemplated pouring a third. Instead he angrily shoved the cork back into the bottle's neck and returned the bottle to its drawer.

'There's nothing much I can tell you, Cantrell. The colonel let you read the reports.'

As if realizing the foolishness of that comment, he looked away from Cantrell sheepishly.

'How much of *that* report was fabricated?'

Griffin shook his head. 'Not much. Didn't think we needed to lie to anyone.'

'Tell me anyway.'

'She's dead, Cantrell. I'm sorry. But see enough death and you build up a tolerance. Men, women, Indians, doesn't matter. It's all ugly and it's all bad. Natural, like hell,' he spat viciously. 'You die, it's just plain bad. It makes a hell of a mess.'

'Mary was stabbed,' Cantrell prompted.

'Yeah. Long knife, wide blade. One blow. Straight through her chest. Split her sternum.'

Griffin looked up at a sound Susan had made.

'Not an Indian knife,' Cantrell said. 'Sounds like a Bowie.'

'Could have got it off a white man,' Griffin snapped, turning away.

'Her feet were cut.'

'Damn it, man, this was your wife. You don't have to know all of this.'

Cantrell went to the desk, reached into the bottom drawer and pulled out the whiskey bottle. He sloshed some of the cloudy liquid into the glass and pushed it at Griffin. The doctor ignored it.

'She'd walked for a while without shoes,' Griffin said, sinking deeper into his chair. 'Maybe as much as a week. She hadn't eaten much, but she'd found water. She didn't have the strength to fight off her attackers when they came, but she did put up a struggle. Bruising on the face and chest showed she'd been punched. Her left cheekbone was broken.' Griffin looked up sharply. 'This what you want to hear?'

'Tell me.'

'They didn't just punch her. They hurt her other ways. Rape. I figure two of them, maybe three from the bruising on her thighs and knees and ankles. Her right knee was dislocated. She was cut across the face, too.'

Susan had followed Cantrell into the room on cat's feet. She had her hands on his shoulders.

'That's enough, Tobias. Let's go.'

'She was lying down when she died?'

'I think so. The blood collects, you see, and. . . .'

'So they just stabbed her?' Cantrell interrupted.

Griffin shook his head. 'Told you she was a fighter. She got a few licks in. I think she got hold of the knife from one of her attackers only to have it used on her. It wasn't there when the patrol found her, though, so I guess they took it back.'

For a long minute the two men stared at each other.

'Your report was vague about the men who killed Susan.'

'Well I wasn't there, was I?' Griffin took the glass of whiskey and drank it down in one swallow. 'I've got to get back home,' he said in a whisper.

'They were white men.' Cantrell glared at the doctor, refusing to release him.

'I think so,' the doctor said, at last. 'Indians would have taken her captive. The dress she was wearing was Indian buckskin so I figure she'd escaped from them.'

'Which white men?'

'I don't know.'

'The man who found her?'

Cantrell ignored Susan's gasp as he fended off Griffin's drunkenly thrown fist. The doctor had come violently to his feet and swung his right hand with all his might. Now breathless, the ageing lieutenant bent over his desk as Cantrell righted the man's chair. Cantrell then eased the doctor back into his seat.

'You bastard. You've no right. I knew Covington. He did his level best to help the woman.'

Nodding, Cantrell said, 'I know he did.'

From behind them, a voice asked, 'Then why ask the question?'

Captain MacArthur stood in the doorway, a slab of granite ready to drop on Cantrell.

'Because it had to be asked. I've some questions of you, too.'

MacArthur held up a hand to stop Cantrell. 'There's

nothing in the reports to suggest that white men killed your wife.'

'There wouldn't be. That would suggest that Covington had been killed by white men, too.'

'I don't see what you're saying.'

Griffin snorted derisively has he poured more whiskey into his glass.

'How did Covington find my wife?'

'A scouting party stumbled on her and alerted Covington, who was in command of the patrol. He tried to save her but she didn't live long.'

'This scouting party, they were part of Covington's patrol?'

'No. They had gone out several days before and were reported missing. They told Covington that they had been dodging Apaches for days.'

'Why did Covington go out to that area again a few days later?'

MacArthur's face tightened.

'Yes, I read the report you gave me,' Cantrell said. 'I'd like to know the truth.'

'That is the truth. He said he wanted to go out in search of those renegades.'

Cantrell could hear hesitation in the captain's voice. 'But?'

'He thought the woman's death was . . . odd. The scouting party reported seeing a band of Apaches riding away from the woman, but Covington wasn't convinced.'

'That wasn't in the report.'

'No.'

'I want to talk to the men who went with him on the patrols.'

'All right.' MacArthur nodded with resignation. 'I'll have Private Wells come see you.'

'What about the rest?'

'Three have been transferred to other posts where the Indian problem is more pressing. Two have been discharged, and one is dead.'

Cantrell felt his stomach cramp with sudden under-standing and hatred.

'The ones who were discharged. Who are they?'

'A couple of foul-ups. They're the ones who got sepa-rated from their patrol and stumbled on your wife. Not army material.'

'Their names,' Cantrell demanded, his voice strained.

'Beckert and Marklin.'

CHAPTER NINE

Marklin fought with his mount, a rebellious bay dusted in charcoal, and tightened the reins on its bobbing head as its long mane snapped like tiny whips. He was a fair horseman, but this animal had given him trouble ever since he bought it. Sidestepping down the trail, Marklin had to crane his neck to see the hoof-marks of Beckert's horse.

It had been Jovane who'd said it, but they both suspected Beckert would foolishly ignore orders and head for the Zunis. Marklin let some time pass after Beckert left, finished his cigar and cognac, then called down for his horse to be saddled and brought around to the hotel.

Marklin followed the north-eastern trail out of town, toward Piñon Creek, following the unmistakable cloud of dust Beckert had kicked up. Twice Marklin stopped to get his bearings. Red Butte to his left, empty plains to his right rimmed by a flat, reddish hill range. When he reached Oatil Creek he paused again, not seeing Beckert's tracks on the opposite side of the narrow stream.

Shaking his head, sneering contemptuously, he turned north-west, spurring the bay into the shallow, sluggish water. The animal didn't like the slick rocks and stumbled often, always fighting to step up onto the grassy collar at the stream's edge. About a hundred yards upstream he found some crushed grass and hoof-prints. He followed these for another mile until he was certain of their course. With a low growl of disdain, he turned the bay about and put it into a gallop. Beckert was a fool, he thought, not for the first time. He'd hired that thug to kill the woman and that had gone badly. Fear had made him do that. Fear and greed. Now he was near panic, and his actions could cost them all their fortunes. For a moment he thought about turning around and chasing after Beckert. Killing him before he could do more harm. But Jovane was a difficult man to read. He didn't like his men taking matters into their own hands. He might commend Marklin for quick thinking, then again he might kill him for not reporting in. Those had been Jovane's last words to him: 'Let me know what he does.'

Marklin left the bay tied to the hitch rail outside the hotel and hurried upstairs. He entered Jovane's room without knocking.

Jovane, smoking a thick, black cigar and with a fresh pot of coffee beside him, looked up and calmly asked, 'Well?'

'As you figured. He didn't go to the Piñon Creek range. He tried to cover his tracks and headed around Red Butte.'

Nodding, Jovane said, 'He'll go into the Zunis and look for Mrs Covington and the stranger.'

To Marklin's surprise Jovane paused a long time to consider this, staring at his cigar as if it held the answer. Then he shook his head.

'Too many questions, if the woman dies,' he said, more to himself than to Marklin. 'Have my horse readied and see to provisions. We may be out there for a few days. I want Beckert stopped before he gets anywhere near those two.'

'What if they find something out there?'

'It's a big range. Besides, what is there to find? No, let them look. Nothing they see will point back to us.'

Marklin turned then stopped abruptly to look back at Jovane. 'What about Beckert's share?'

Jovane smiled coldly. 'Why, we split it, of course. There'll be only the two of us left. That ought to assuage any guilt you might have for killing your cousin.'

Marklin didn't smile. His face had become like stone. 'I don't feel no guilt. He's a damned fool and deserves what's coming.'

Private Frank Wells stared at the camp-fire, his jaw quivering, his eyes locked on the flames in desperate hope that the man would not bark at him again. They had been out two days and Cantrell's orneriness was growing. They were not making particularly good time, and it was due to Mrs Covington. She was a good rider, Wells had decided, though unaccustomed to the wilderness. The young private had tried to help her as much as he could, but she was one to do for herself. She was mighty pretty, far too young to be a widow, and if Cantrell was a little friendlier Wells might be able to sneak a few more glances at her.

Their supper finished, and dishes scrubbed clean, Cantrell stalked off to the edge of the firelight.

'How much further?' he asked.

'We should reach the spot by tomorrow. We'll know it by the angle of the rocks. Only patch of 'em in this part of the plain.'

They had spent much of the first day climbing the sloping north face of the Zunis, and the second crossing large grassy meadows or wending through dense forests of piñon and, higher up, tall Ponderosa pine. They had seen no one. Occasionally in the clearings they could see sign of Indian camps, but these were old. To the south there were craggy rises, misty in the distance, which sometimes peaked above the tree-line, denoting the sheer southern lip of the Zunis.

'And this is the way your patrol came?'

'Both times, give or take a few hundred yards,' Wells said, shrugging an apology. 'Out here there aren't many landmarks. I remember we headed for Dagger Head, and that's the trail we're on now.'

Wells had pointed out Dagger Head when they moved out of the trees. It was a tall, craggy peak, narrow and stained with red rock at the southern edge of the range. They could see the tip of it as they rode, and Wells kept them in line with it.

Like the night before, Cantrell took the first watch. After a time, Susan joined him, standing close and resting her head on his shoulder. His left shoulder, Wells noted, leaving his gun hand free.

The next morning they rode out early, the tall grass moist with dew and the air cold and still. By mid-morning they found a narrow stream and stopped to water the horses and refill their canteens. They ate a quick breakfast of left-over biscuits and jerked beef.

They had been moving steadily higher as they passed through thickets of aspen and Douglas fir. Dagger Head disappeared from view. When they emerged from the forest more than an hour later, the ominous peak loomed large over distant treetops. They were at the edge of another wide, downward sloping meadow of wild grass and juniper bushes. The occasional stand of loosely bunched aspen dotted the sweeping plain. Two miles south lay a jagged clump of rock that clung like a bloody scab to the soft grass skin of the valley. Five miles or more beyond the rock was a thick pine forest that stretched across the width of the horizon and climbed up the rugged south rim of the Zunis.

At the tree-line Cantrell called a halt to study the valley. There was no movement to be seen other than a few deer loping carelessly in the tall grass.

'That's the rocks,' Wells said, pointing.

They reached the site at a trot a few minutes later. The rocks were as unusual as Wells had said. They rose straight out of the ground but looked as if they had been sheared by a rough chisel at a forty-five degree angle. Bloody streaks of iron gave them a gory appearance. A bare collar of hard-packed sand ringed the odd-shaped boulders unevenly. From what Cantrell could see, this clump extended several hundred yards in each direction. A myriad of shadowed passageways presented between the rocks.

Cantrell got off his horse and looked around for a moment, uncertain. 'Show me,' he said to Wells, after a time.

Wells dismounted smartly and led his coal-black gelding around a low-shouldered boulder to a small alcove. He looked around studiously, nodding, as if seeing the nondescript bit of sand and rock confirmed his memory.

'This is it. The woman was . . .' Abruptly, he stopped speaking and looked up at Cantrell.

'Go ahead.' His voice was laced with impatience.

'Your wife was lying here. I came around with Lieutenant Covington and got a clear look at her.'

'She was dead.'

Wells gave a tentative shake of his head. 'No. But she was slipping fast. She was grabbing at her bloody shirt, but there was nothing there.'

Susan stepped into the alcove, her eyes locked on Cantrell.

'How'd you find her?'

Wells pointed to a charred section of ground. 'There was a fire going and we spotted the smoke. The lieutenant thought it best to investigate.'

Cantrell stepped over to a patch of ground that had been turned. Someone had used a shovel to dig out a hole. They hadn't gotten far. The hole wasn't deep enough for something to have been buried there.

'What about this?' Cantrell asked.

'Beckert was digging when we found him.'

Raw anger flushed over Cantrell's face. 'A grave? While she was still alive?'

Wells swallowed hard and nodded. 'She didn't live long, mister. A few minutes is all.'

'Go on. Don't make me drag it out of you, Private.'

'Marklin was next to your wife. His shirt was bloody and he kind of looked shaken. Lieutenant Covington asked what happened and Marklin said they had heard the woman scream and found her on the ground, dying. They tried to help her and built a fire, they said, but figured out pretty quick that she wasn't going to make it. That's when Beckert started digging the grave.' Wells looked away from Cantrell's hot stare.

'Did Covington believe them?'

After a moment Wells shrugged. 'He didn't say nothing, but he was angry. He dismounted and tried to help your wife, but she died right about then. I remember him staring at Beckert and Marklin for a long time. Then he called for a blanket and had your wife wrapped up in it and laid her across his saddle. Said they'd bury her proper.'

Susan started crying, softly. She turned away and sat on a rock.

'What reason did Beckert and Marklin give for being there?'

'They'd gotten lost on a patrol. They'd gone out with Lieutenant Gleason a couple of days before we went out and got separated. They said they'd been chased by Indians for three days.'

'And they figured an Indian had killed her? Did they see any around?'

'No. But . . .' Wells looked around suddenly then darted toward a small rock. He reached behind it and drew out a broken lance. It was worn, the feathers split and dirty, the dyed red rawhide strips now pale. The elements had dulled what had been a bright ceremonial instrument of war.

Cantrell took the lance, his face souring. 'This was their proof of Indian attack, I take it.'

'That's what they said. They'd seen a small raiding party of four braves riding west.'

'Had you seen the braves?'

Wells shrugged apologetically. 'We wouldn't have. These rocks would have blocked our view.'

Cantrell paced slowly for a few minutes, staring at the ground and worrying the smooth wood of the lance. In disgust, he tossed aside the useless pieces.

'You were sent out to find Gleason's patrol?'

'No, sir. Lieutenant Gleason had orders to patrol the western plateaux and Lieutenant Covington the eastern, but, well, Lieutenant Gleason's compass don't work so well most times.'

'He wandered.'

'Yes, sir. We met him on his way back just on the other side of that last forest we passed through. He asked us to be on the look out for Beckert and Marklin. Hell, other than Lieutenant Gleason, those were the lostest two men I ever did meet.'

'Captain MacArthur told me they were both foul-ups and that they were drummed out of the service.'

Again, Wells shrugged. 'They weren't particularly good soldiers, I expect. And when they left few men cared.'

This piqued Cantrell's interest. 'Who did care?'

'Howard Dundee, mostly. He and Beckert and Marklin were tight. There were a couple of others: Blevins and Sokalov.'

'Are they still in the service?'

'Blevins and Sokalov were transferred to Company D stationed in Oklahoma at Fort Sill. Dundee is dead.'

'Indians?'

Wells lowered his head and shook it. 'Accident on guard duty during midnight watch. He was kind of lazy and would nap in the cannon barricade. A wheel came loose and a cannon crushed his head.'

Suspicion darkened Cantrell's face. 'Who was the other guard on duty at that post?'

'Marklin.'

Listening to the men, Susan began to feel a chill creep

through her. Cantrell's questions were telling her a story even more than Wells's answers.

'When my husband came back here,' she asked, 'Marklin and Beckert were with him?'

'Yes, ma'am. So was I. Lieutenant Gleason said he was tired of dealing with those two and Captain MacArthur reassigned them.'

The voices were dim and distant, and the rocks bounced the sound around so it was impossible to tell from which direction they came. Fidgeting nervously, Beckert inched up the long, shallow slope of a great boulder, pausing every foot or so to listen. These were human voices, but he couldn't make out what they were saying or who was speaking. It had to be the stranger and the Covington woman. There was a third voice, too. Younger, higher-pitched, often hard to hear. Well, it wasn't the colonel or Captain MacArthur, that's for certain, Beckert thought. The old walrus and MacArthur could be heard whispering at a hundred paces in a rainstorm. They must have assigned the stranger a guide.

He crawled to the top of the boulder and very slowly raised his head to look around. He was at the edge of the boulder-field, his horse picketed below. Before him were the ragged tops of chiseled rock and a few rounded faces of basalt mounds. Dark, shallow canyons cracked through the rock like veins of a broken pane of glass. He saw no movement below nor was it any clearer from which direction came the voices.

Frustrated, Beckert eased down the far side of the boulder and jumped to another across a three-foot divide. He stumbled over an indentation larger than his boot and, curious, gave it quick attention. It was an imprint, a foot from some ancient animal with three toes. From there he scuttled like a spider along the tops of the rocks, pausing occasionally to listen. The sound ebbed and flowed and his inability to pin-point the speakers maddened him. He became careless. Some loose stones skittered down the side of the boulder as his boot scraped against them, and rattled noisily. Fear gripping his gut, Beckert froze. The feathery voices, though, didn't stop. They hadn't heard.

A hundred yards away, however, more careful hands and feet paused. Hidden in the shadows between the rocks the sound of skittering stones echoed softly toward them. Dark eyes turned toward the ridges above, scanning for movement. A hand eased down toward the Colt holstered around a narrow waist.

Susan dried her eyes and took a long, slow breath. Cantrell had stalked off to stare down the thin corridors of the boulder field. Not knowing what else to do, Private Wells went for the horses and walked them into a small break in the rocks where he picketed them to forage on meager tufts of dry grass. He then climbed to the top of a roughly chiseled hunk of stone, out to its precarious peak, and craned his neck toward the west. After a moment he hopped down and vigorously brushed dust from his dark uniform.

'The sun will set in a while. If we want to start heading back we'd best get started.'

'No,' Cantrell said. 'I want to explore this field.'

Wells blanched. 'But Captain MacArthur said—'

'I don't care what he told you. Head back if you want. My wife was killed here and I'm going to look around.'

Susan put a gentle hand on the young private's shoulder. 'It's too late to go now. Why don't you get some firewood.'

Grateful for something to do, Wells scampered about picking up deadfall and bringing it back to the charred ground where the previous camp-fire had burned itself out. Susan went to Cantrell and pressed up against him. He didn't pull away. In a moment she could feel the tension in his body ease.

'What do you expect to find?' she asked, softly.

'I don't know.'

Her voice trembled a little as she said, 'They killed her, didn't they? Marklin and Beckert.' He nodded. 'And they killed William too.'

That question he left unanswered. He turned to Wells, who had already put together a neat pile of wood that would last them the night. He sure was an efficient soldier, Cantrell thought.

'Tell me about your second patrol. Who ordered that?'

Wells shrugged. 'I don't know. I figured it was Captain MacArthur. But then there were only five of us, and that's not much of a force to go hunting Indians, especially if they was in a killing mood.'

'How'd you get picked?'

'The lieutenant chose me, like the others.' Wells removed his cap and scratched his head. 'Tell the truth I didn't expect Marklin to be ordered on that patrol.'

'Who were the others?'

'Corporal Gilbert and Private Stovall. I don't reckon either of 'em knew what they was in the middle of.'

'But you did?' Cantrell said, eagerly.

Wells nodded. 'I guess I did. You could feel the lieutenant's anger and it only got stronger the longer we was out.'

'Anger at who?'

'Marklin,' Wells said after some hesitation. 'The lieutenant sure didn't trust him. Kept him close all the time. Rode side by side the whole way, and kept looking over at him. Never let Markin get behind him. Made him edgy.'

'What were *your* orders?'

'The lieutenant just said we were going out to look for that raiding party.'

'Where did you go?'

'That's just it, we didn't go nowhere but here. Made a beeline and the lieutenant set a fast pace. We came right to this spot, just like now, and then the lieutenant started down these paths.'

'Alone?' Susan asked.

'At first. We were all standing around looking for braves. We didn't see none. After a few minutes he came out and split us into two units. He took Marklin and Stovall and I went with Gilbert.'

Susan was visibly tensing now as Wells recounted her husband's last minutes of life.

'We were out about ten minutes. For a bit we could hear the lieutenant and the others making their way through the various passages. They'd get closer to us and then further away. Then it went quiet. It was about then that I heard movement up on the rocks above. Gilbert had the idea to mark our way with an X scratched into the rock so we could find the path back to our horses. We had just started back when we heard a yelp like someone got surprised. Then there were three shots real quick in a row and then another.

'Gilbert and I double-timed it back to the horses, then found the passage the lieutenant had taken. We weren't fifty feet down it when Marklin runs up and says we have to get back to the horses. He looks kind of wild and his uniform is torn along the arm.'

'What about William?' Susan asked.

'I tried to squeeze past Marklin, ma'am, I truly did. He said the lieutenant ordered us back to the fort for reinforcements. There were just too many Indians to fight off with just us three. I asked about the lieutenant and Marklin said that he was a goner and going fast but that he'd hold off the bunch of them while we rode out.'

Cantrell ignored Susan's quiet tears. 'What about Stovall?'

'Later Marklin said that Stovall got took by them Indians.'

'Did *you* see any Indians?'

'I did. Honestly. Two of 'em were creeping along the rocks kind of where we'd heard some sounds and I took a shot. I think I hit him 'cause he dropped hard. Anyway, getting to our horses I heard more shots, which I took to be the lieutenant's gun, and one or two which were rifle shots. We rode off fast and didn't look back.'

'But you never did see any more Indians, did you? Just those two.'

The sternness in Cantrell's voice made Wells shrink a bit. 'No, sir.'

'You came back with the rescue party?'

'Me and Marklin both.'

Cantrell had read the report of that patrol. They'd found Covington hacked up, shot in the back, and no Indians anywhere, although there was a large bloodstain on a rock about ten feet from Covington's body. There were several fresh chips shot out of the rocks around the body where bullets had hit. Lieutenant Bartoth, leading the patrol, questioned Marklin about Covington's wound. Marklin said that they had been attacked from behind. Bartoth found the story to be plausible and wrote it up that way.

'No one questioned Marklin after they got back to the fort?' Susan asked, her voice thin, almost desperate.

'He was in with the captain and the colonel both, ma'am. I guess,' he added apologetically, 'they didn't find nothing wrong with his story. But it wasn't long after that he and Beckert were drummed out.'

She didn't have to ask Wells if he believed Marklin. The young private looked stricken. Hearing it all laid out in front of him made the truth of it plain to him. The thought dawning on him was written large across his guileless face.

'Sir, what's out here that's worth killing over? And why kill a woman who'd've been half-dead running from Indians?'

'She thought she'd found rescuers,' he muttered to himself, angrily. 'What's out here?' he asked suddenly.

'Nothing! That's what I don't get,' Wells said. 'No towns or nothing. This is all government land, is what I understand.'

'Beckert and Marklin were out here for a reason. We've some daylight left. Show me the passage Lieutenant Covington took.'

Wells jumped forward and pointed to a narrow, angled slit between two large boulders. Cantrell tilted his upper body and eased himself through. Several yards further in the crack widened and Cantrell was able to stand straight. Behind him came Wells and Susan.

The path was not marked, but for a hundred feet or so there was only one direction to follow. The way opened up into a ten-foot-square patch of sand from which two more passages led. Anticipating Cantrell, Wells shot a hand out, pointing toward the left. Again the passage narrowed and then widened. Several other, narrower corridors opened as they slowly wended their way through the rock field. Cantrell's eyes went everywhere, taking in everything, but his face was sour with dissatisfaction.

When the way narrowed again, Cantrell chose to take a wider side path, and very quickly this one dumped into a deep circular dead end. He knew immediately that this was where Covington had died, and so did Susan. Numbly, she walked forward to a small boulder against the far wall which was stained brown with dried blood. Cantrell scanned the walls and saw the stone chipped by rifle bullets. It was exactly as Marklin had reported.

Could he be wrong, Cantrell wondered, about Marklin and Beckert? No. Those two were bad news, of that he was certain. Bile rose up in his throat. They could never be tried in court, and killing them in cold blood would only make him an outlaw. He might be able to get Beckert to draw against him, but Marklin wouldn't budge. Not unless the odds were heavily in his favor. Then there was the mystery man who seemed to hold Marklin's leash. Cantrell had spotted him in the Dog's Leg, quiet, coy, with intelligent eyes and a devil's grin. Where did he fit into this?

None of them heard the scrape of boot against rock, so intent were they on their own thoughts. The shot rang out like a cannon blast in that tight canyon, making all three jump. Cantrell whirled, drawing his Colt, and fired at the sound of their attacker. His bullet pinged wildly off the rocks and ricocheted back into the close canyon. Susan screamed. Someone was on the rounded boulder above them, lifting to one knee. He fired again and Cantrell could feel the tug of something against his sleeve. A third shot missed as the man tried to shift position to get more cover. Cantrell sighted carefully and squeezed off a cartridge. The man jolted to a stop. His boot-heel caught against a ridge and he stumbled even as he turned to fire again. Cantrell loosed another round, striking the man in the chest. He was done for then, and collapsed. Almost instantly his body began to slip forward along the smooth stone and with a sickening thud slammed to the ground.

Cantrell ran to him, grabbing his gun. It was Beckert and he was dead.

'Tobias!' Susan cried hoarsely.

He whirled toward her to find her kneeling beside the body of Private Wells.

CHAPTER TEN

The kid was still breathing. Beckert's first bullet had punched a hole in Wells's side just below the ribs. He was grimacing, holding his face tight, trying not to cry out. Susan took the kerchief from around his neck and pressed it against the wound.

'We can't stay,' Cantrell said, grabbing Wells under the left arm.

Angry, Susan said, 'You can't move him!'

'We have to. Beckert didn't come alone.'

They could all hear the sound of boots thumping on rock now. Wells got to his feet, his whole body shaking, and tried to lean on Cantrell. Instead, Cantrell pushed him toward Susan.

'Get back to the horses,' he said.

'He can't ride!'

'He won't have to. Not yet.'

Forcing a grin, Wells said, 'Come on, ma'am, before the real shootin' starts.'

Cantrell crossed to Beckert's body and began to draw it out of sight. He got the corpse into the narrow passage then noticed that something was on the ground where the body had lain. A tiny leather pouch drawn tight with a rawhide string. Quickly, he retrieved it and was almost to the safety of the passage when a figure loomed above the rocks. Cantrell threw a snap shot up at the man as he ducked into the break in the rock. Three booming shots chased him.

Ahead he saw Susan and Wells struggling to make their way to the horses. Susan glanced back at him, her eyes wide with fear. Cantrell waved at her silently to keep moving.

Two shots bounced along the rocks after him, spraying shards down on his head. Cantrell spun around and fired down the passage. A voice yelped with surprise. Cantrell fired two more shots, aiming low this time, but blindly. He heard someone in hushed tones say, 'Get back, damn it!'

Susan and Wells were out of sight now. Soon they'd be out of the boulder field and by the horses.

Without seeing these new attackers Cantrell knew that Marklin was one of them. Marklin and another man had jumped down into the canyon after him and were now stuck. He could climb out, and perhaps his partner was doing just that, but he couldn't do it without exposing his back.

Cantrell chased the wind with another shot.

Night was falling quickly as thick clouds cut off the sun. In another hour it would be pitch-black. Slowly a plan formed in Cantrell's mind. Much of it depended on Wells. The boy had shown some brass. Cantrell hoped he had a deep reserve of it.

Over the next five minutes he fired shots every minute and in-between listened for movement down the canyon. By now they would be certain that Cantrell was not advancing on them. They'd risk climbing out, even if more shots were fired.

Cantrell reached down and removed his spurs, pocketing them for later, then eased backward down the passage. In the dimming light he backtrailed to the crooked rocks and slipped out into the open. Wells lay on the ground, looking pale and perspiring. Susan had taken one of their canteens and set about cleaning the soldier's wound. They both looked up at him, afraid, expectant, when he appeared and started building a fire.

Whispering, Susan said, 'They'll see the light and smoke.'

'I'm counting on it.'

Once the fire was going he scouted around and found several small trees. He tore off green branches. These he dropped onto the fire and within a few minutes great clouds of smoke began pouring out. Cantrell then took one of his spurs, broke off the small rowel, and shoved the shank into the flames.

'Are you trying to get us killed?'

'They'd find us soon enough, Susan. I want them to think we're not going anywhere. That way they'll take their time attacking. Probably wait until dark.'

'We can't go anywhere unless we leave Private Wells behind.'

'I'll hold 'em off, sir.' Wells's voice was none too eager.

'I've another plan. But it means you'll travel tonight.'

Wells looked down at the bloody hole in his side. 'I'm not sure I can get far like this.'

'I know,' Cantrell said gravely. As gently as he could he rolled Wells over on to his right side and tore back his blood-soaked uniform. The bullet had gone through. At least they'd had that bit of luck.

Using his kerchief, Cantrell adjusted the placement of the spur in the fire. Wells saw what he was doing and shivered. He looked up at Cantrell, his eyes wet. Slowly, he nodded.

'I guess I know what you're thinking,' he said.

'Don't be afraid to cry out, Private.'

'Not to worry, sir. I won't make a sound.'

Cantrell pulled the spur out of the fire. The shank glowed a dull reddish black. 'Look, kid, I want you to. Scream loud and long. Let it out.'

'But they'll hear me.'

'That's what I want. I want them to know we've a wounded man who can't travel.'

'They'll pick us off if they find us.'

'We'll be gone long before they move in for the kill. Now scream, damn it.'

Cantrell jammed the hot iron against Wells's back wound. Despite orders, the young soldier tried to hold back his scream but finally gave in as Cantrell bore down. Susan stared at him hotly, shaking with silent rage.

Cantrell returned the shank to the fire then rolled Wells onto his back. The boy was groggy. His skin had gone clammy and nearly translucent. Cantrell held his head while giving him a drink from the canteen.

'I scream loud enough?' Wells asked, trembling.

'Almost. That was the tough one. We need to cauterize the wound in front. You can rest for a bit after that, but then we'll have to mount up.'

'Yes, sir.'

Cantrell applied the hot shank a second time. Wells moaned and his eyes started to roll up in his head. By

145

sheer will he kept himself from passing out and forced himself to scream. When he was done, Cantrell angrily tossed aside the spur and left the ring of light, flipping his Colt into his hand.

Susan used more water to wash Wells's face. Looking down at the wound nearly sickened her. The smell of burned flesh hung in the air.

'It'll be fine, now, ma'am.'

She nodded. 'I know.'

In a dark corner, Cantrell took the pouch Beckert had dropped and opened it. Inside were raw stones. Ore. He poured them into his left hand and watched as the glow of the fire reflected dully off the silvery-gray veins in the rock. It made sense now, he thought, feeling a wave of sadness wash over him, strangely muting his anger. He had his answers now, and Susan's, too.

When the attack came, it came with gunfire. The shots echoed in the still night like distant hammers. Susan pulled up sharply and turned in her saddle, looking back over her shoulder. She could no longer see their camp-fire. Cantrell, one hand under Wells's left arm, kept the young soldier in the saddle as they rode.

'We need to pick up the pace,' he said.

The wounded man turned toward him, not much more than a shadow against the black night. 'I'll be all right.'

Wells had had no more than half an hour to rest before Cantrell silently roused them and led them out of camp. Once shrouded in blackness they mounted and eased away from the rocks, letting the grass muffle the horses' steps. Cantrell had pointed them directly south. He wanted to get through the forest ahead and up into the hills. He'd be able to find a place where Wells could rest, where Susan could look after him, before he went back to hunt down their pursuers.

Susan had wanted to try to make it back to Fort Wingate. It was too far; Wells and Cantrell insisted on that. And the trip would leave them out in the open, vulnerable. In the hills they would have the high ground and protection. Cantrell wondered about Wells's eagerness to head south toward the precipitous edge of the Zuni range. But he realized that, skinny and frail-looking as he was, the young soldier was a fighter. He was looking to get a pound of flesh back from those who shot him.

Gigging their horses, they sped up into a canter. The swishing of the grass as they passed sounded harsh and loud in Cantrell's ears, but he knew the sound wouldn't carry far. Marklin and the man holding his strings wouldn't hear them. With the night in full bloom, and no moon to speak of, they wouldn't be able to pick out tracks. By morning most of the grass, bent by their passing, would spring back, leaving no sign of their crossing. Unless Marklin or the other man were an expert tracker. They might be able to pick out some sign. Cantrell had tried to cover their trail, but running as they were and with keeping Wells among the living, there was little more he could do.

He had judged the forest to be no more than five miles from the rocks. Using his inner compass, Cantrell led them due south. The horses maintained a steady pace, Cantrell slowing occasionally to conserve their energy, and they reached the line of trees in under two hours. Cantrell pulled up at the trees and dismounted. He offered to help Wells down.

'No, sir. If I get down out of the saddle I won't be going back up.'

Cantrell accepted this. He passed water around and decided not to spend much time there. Within ten minutes he and Susan were mounted again, and the three of them were moving.

Eventually, the sunrise cut through the trees as they made their way uphill through the forest of pine, aspen, and fir. The woods were thick with the heady smells of wet needles and leaves waking as the spring sun began to warm the ground. Still, the air was crisp and its bite was making Wells shiver. The young soldier began to wobble in the saddle. Cantrell had to ride stirrup to stirrup to keep leverage on him.

Susan had given up her constant vigil behind them. Her face was set with grim determination, mixed with anger. The shock of what happened had worn off. Now she was mad.

They broke through the trees by mid-morning to find the sun full and bright and warm. Before them were twisted rises of bare rock bubbling up in different directions and to various heights. Rough talus lay at the base of these rises, and above them were dangerous peaks of weather-honed basalt. Dagger Head stood to their right in bloody grandeur.

Cantrell scanned the ridges looking for a place to hide. There seemed no way up into the rocks. They turned west and rode for several miles until they stood almost directly below Dagger Head. The ground had lifted considerably and the horses took the climb easily. But Wells didn't have much time. He wobbled in the saddle uncontrollably, only Cantrell's strong right arm keeping him from collapsing.

At the top of the rise they paused again for Cantrell to look around.

'Tobias,' Susan said, urgently. He looked at her to see she was pointing down into the valley below. They were up high enough to see over the tops of the trees. Two riders were off to the east and south of the rocks a little way. But they weren't moving. After a few moments, they started away from their position and rode hard and fast toward Dagger Head.

'OK,' Cantrell said. 'They've spotted us. We wanted that, anyway.'

'Better to fight,' Wells said, his voice weak.

'Still,' Cantrell said, noting Susan's worried expression, 'we need to get you to a safe place. Looks like there's a game trail along this rise up and around Dagger Head.'

Wells opened his eyes and blinked several times to clear them. He stared at the beaten path leading off the rise and into the rugged, bare hills.

'That's no game trail,' he said, shaking his head. 'Men rode that way.'

'Two men at least.' Cantrell ignored Susan's questioning look. With a touch of his heels he got them all moving up the trail and toward the bloody edge of Dagger Head.

Marklin examined the ground. The rocky, dry soil didn't hold prints very well. He stood up and looked around, studying the distances around him for a clue to where the stranger and the others had gone.

'Well,' he said at length, 'they were here. Just not sure where they headed.'

'Of course they were here,' Jovane said, his voice dripping with disdain. 'We saw them. This is the only rise for miles around high enough to be seen from the valley.'

'I say we split up,' Marklin offered. It might help them find the others quicker, and it would certainly get him away from the annoyingly superior Jovane.

'There's only one place they could have gone,' Jovane said, stepping his gelded roan toward the narrow trail leading up toward Dagger Head.

Marklin grinned darkly. 'Fine. Let 'em go up there. They'll have to come down sooner or later or starve to death. There's just about no way down the other side for twenty miles. And with that wounded soldier in tow, they'll never make it. We'll wait here.'

Jovane's disgust was thick and undisguised. 'I suppose you want them to find the cave.'

'It don't matter,' Marklin said with a shrug. 'They won't get past us.'

Jovane wasn't so sure. That stranger was a smart one, and good with his guns. Jovane didn't like being in the open with a man like that able to shoot down on him from the rocks above. The stranger was driven and at last Jovane knew why. He had talked to the hotel clerk and got the stranger's name. He had a friend or two at the fort and they told him Cantrell had been looking for his wife, kidnapped by Indians, and left for dead in the Zunis. It had to be the same woman dressed in Indian garb whom Marklin had killed. Riding out to the Zunis Jovane had considered simply killing Marklin and leaving him for the wolves. But it was too late for that now. The stranger, Tobias Cantrell, was too far down the trail. If they could have stopped Beckert in time things might have been different. Hell, if Beckert had just not fallen into that little box canyon after Jovane shot him they could have ridden away in safety. Cantrell would have had his suspicions but no proof. Now he had proof, enough of it at least to keep digging. And Cantrell was heading right for the one place that would ruin their entire operation. He had to be stopped. All of them had to die. Especially Marklin.

They reached the bottom of the slope still edging along the narrow trail. After a time the path widened and Cantrell was able to pull Wells's horse alongside.

'How are you doing, Private?' The soldier, tied to his saddle, was slumped over the horn. His skin had taken on a sickly shade of gray.

'Holding on, sir.'

Cantrell sensed Susan glaring at him from behind. She knew the boy couldn't last much longer. He ignored her – and his own qualms about the strange turns the trail had taken, and kept his eyes on the ground. He didn't believe for a moment that the trail would take them to the valley floor. It would end somewhere ahead and trap them. Before then he hoped to find what he was looking for.

Ten minutes later he reined up and dismounted to examine the tracks he'd been following for the past hour.

'We can't linger,' Susan said. 'Those men will catch up with us.'

'We have time.' He stood and looked around. There were several breaks in the jagged walls that rose above them. They had seen caves all along the trail and he had been tempted to stop and let Wells rest. But none of them appeared very deep nor did they offer a place to conceal their horses. The one he saw now was different. It was rounder and higher and just inside he could see thick timbers supporting the entrance.

Cantrell quickly untied Wells, caught him as he fell, and carried him into the cave. Susan followed, bringing with her blankets and water. Once inside she stopped short and gasped.

'Someone lives here,' she said.

'Now and again,' Cantrell agreed.

On the walls were several torches, black with recent use. Deeper into the cave – more a tunnel, really – he found a bed of straw, a lantern, and a fire-pit ringed by round, blackened stones. He placed Wells on the bed then stepped out of the way to let Susan begin her work.

'A mine?' Wells asked meekly.

Cantrell lit a torch while Susan ignited the lantern. 'A silver-mine. Beckert and Marklin, and whoever else is riding with them, have been working on it. I found a pouch of silver ore in Beckert's clothes back at the rocks.'

'And it's on army land,' Wells said.

'Yeah. Which is why they're willing to kill anyone who gets close to it. Legally, they can't make a claim so they have to mine it in secret.'

Susan looked up, her face taut with anger. 'William found out about it?'

'He didn't have to. All he had to do was investigate. He was already suspicious of Beckert and Marklin because of their unexplained absences. When he found them with Mary he knew they were lying.'

Wells nodded as he lay back after drinking from the canteen. 'They were coming here to work the mine.'

'Them and a few others. I'll bet those that were killed were in on it.'

'That's why that big man tried to kill us,' Susan said, shivering a little from the shock of it.

'Kill *you*,' Cantrell corrected. 'They didn't know a thing about me. My wife didn't have a name that they knew. She was just a white squaw to them, an escaped captive whose death they could blame on Indians. But you,' he added, 'they didn't want you investigating your husband's death.'

'So what do we do now?'

'Take care of Wells. I'll see to the horses and then go back for Marklin and his keeper. Whoever that man is, he's been pulling the strings on the whole operation.'

'Did he kill William?' Susan's voice was icy.

'No. That was Marklin. But it wouldn't surprise me to learn he ordered William killed.'

She stood up and very stiffly walked to Cantrell. 'Let them come, Tobias. Let them find us so I can kill that man.'

Hearing those cold words from her made his stomach turn. He knew the hatred she felt. He had felt it, too – for years. But that was gone. These men coming for them had to die, and they would because they wouldn't allow for any other choice. But he couldn't let Susan do it. He didn't want her living with the guilt that would follow when the heat of her anger faded.

He took her in his arms and held her to his chest. She stood stiffly in his embrace for several minutes before her body softened. Then she buried her face into his shoulder and quietly began sobbing. After a few minutes she looked up at him. In that instant he wanted to kiss her, to hold her even closer, not in a comforting embrace but as lovers.

Pushing back her tears with his hand he said, 'I'll be back for you.'

He let her go and turned from the mine. Quickly he removed the saddles from two of their horses and brought

153

them and the supplies tied to them inside. He put these near Wells. Already the young soldier was regaining some color and strength. He had taken his service revolver out of its holster and was checking the loads. Cantrell dropped a rifle next to him. With a slight grin, Wells nodded and said. 'Go on. She'll be fine.'

Cantrell didn't look back as he left the mine, swung into the saddle and, with the reins of the other horses in hand, headed down trail.

He had gone about a hundred yards when part of the trail broke off into a shallow *rincón* shrouded in tall, rough grass. After quick inspection he decided to leave the two horses there, tethered to stunted juniper bushes. The *rincón* wouldn't hide the animals for long, but they would be safe for a few hours. If he didn't make it back, Susan and Wells wouldn't need them.

Further ahead, the trail narrowed and began to rise. His horse balked skittishly as the path shrank to less than five feet wide. Cantrell reined up and looked up along the jagged walls. There might be a hint of a ledge up there, he thought. A place he could reach on foot. Below him was a sheer drop of several hundred feet to a jagged bench, and then another drop into mist.

Having decided his course he backed his mount along the trail until he could safely turn the animal. A few minutes later he guided his horse into the *rincón* and hitched him to a juniper bush like the others. He took the rifle from its boot, an extra box of shells from his saddle-bags, and a canteen, and then ran back up the trail.

The path narrowed as he ran. Eventually he was forced to slow to a walk and then to turn his back to the wall as the ledge shrank to less than two feet wide. He had been going up the ever-rising slope for fifteen minutes when a boulder, growing out of the rugged precipice blocked his way.

Above him was the ledge he had spotted earlier. He slid the rifle muzzle down the back of his shirt to secure it and slipped the canteen's rawhide strap around his neck. Then he began climbing hand over hand up the barbed escarpment. Gaining the ledge, one even narrower than the one below, he began working back the way he had come. He wanted to get above the mine entrance, or even further up the trail by the time Marklin and his boss started down it. He had no doubts that they would seek to protect their treasure.

The ledge widened slightly and remained level. Several times ragged fingers of rock cut across it and Cantrell had to pull himself around these, hanging desperately over the void. At the *rincón*, the ledge narrowed considerably and lifted at a precarious angle. Cantrell clung to every outcropping he could grab and with white, sweating fingers he pulled himself to the far side where the ledge widened again, barely.

At last he stood above the mine entrance. He had a clear view up and down the trail for a few hundred yards. He saw no one. But he did see that the ledge on which he was standing ended 200 feet uptrail. He was in a bad position, and knew it. Again he climbed, using the ragged structure of the escarpment to grab handholds and kick away loose rock with his boots to make footholds.

Breathless, he pulled himself up to a wide bench fifty feet uptrail from the mine entrance. He paused to catch his breath and to drink from the canteen. He was in a good spot, but he saw a better. A break in the rock revealed a path leading up in a leisurely slope to the back of Dagger Head. From there he would have a commanding view of the area and plenty of cover.

His hands were raw from climbing, but that wouldn't interfere with his firing the rifle. He pulled it out of his shirt, wiped the sweat from the barrel, and checked the loads. The path he found to be well-trod and strictly confined by rock walls four and five feet high. For the first twenty feet it rose sharp and straight, then the path began to cut left and right, sometimes with severe turns. Cantrell paused after a few minutes, thinking he'd heard a horse. He had started to lift himself up one of the side walls to get a better view of the trail below when a thumping sound alerted him. He dropped from the wall and turned just as a rifle butt slammed into his nose.

Cantrell dropped like a rag-doll and slid backwards down the path. By a stroke of luck he kept hold of his rifle and managed to swing it up as his attacker cut down on him with the butt of his own rifle. The walnut stocks crashed together and the other shattered, creating a shower of wooden shards. Cantrell heard the attacker scream as a large splinter pierced his cheek and blood began running down his neck.

His fingers numb from the shock of the blow, Cantrell fumbled trying to lift his own rifle even as he scrambled to one knee. The attacker kicked wildly with his boot and sent Cantrell's rifle flying down the path, then kicked again, driving lancing pain through Cantrell's chest. Breathless, Cantrell looked up at the man. He recognized him as Marklin's keeper. But Marklin didn't seem to be around.

Jovane grabbed Cantrell's shirt-front and jabbed a

balled fist into his bloody nose. Cantrell felt his legs tremble and weaken. Laughing, Jovane shoved Cantrell mightily and sent him skidding down the path onto the bench. Cantrell's mind reeled as he fought for balance. He felt himself sliding but couldn't stop his wild plummet. His legs slipped over the side of the bench as his hand fell on the discarded rifle. He dangled there above the abyss as Jovane approached slowly. The rifle butt had wedged between rocks and was the only thing keeping Cantrell from plunging to his death.

Jovane kept laughing, even as he yanked the splinter from his cheek. He started to pull the Colt from the holster at his hip, then had second thoughts. Instead, he would boot Cantrell in the head and send him crashing to the rocks below.

Cantrell groaned, weak as a kitten. His grip was loosening and he couldn't pull himself to safety. Stupidly, he had grabbed the rifle with his right hand. Jovane saw this and laughed again. His legs flailing, Cantrell's feet suddenly found a foothold. He lifted up slightly, let go the rifle with his right hand, and reached out to take it with his left. Jovane mistook the move as one made by a man starting to fall to his death and panicking to hold on for one more moment of life.

Too late he realized that Cantrell was not falling but going for his gun. Frantically now, he pulled at his own revolver, desperate to clear the weapon from its leather. He fired before aiming then stumbled backward and fired again. Both shots missed. With steady motions, Cantrell leveled his gun and shot a neat hole in the middle of Jovane's forehead. Jovane toppled forward, instantly dead, the back of his head a mess of blood and brain-matter.

Cantrell's limbs were sapped of strength. Desperately he pulled himself back up to the bench and sat in the lee of a large rock, his body trembling with fatigue. After a minute he reached out and grabbed the rifle, his right hand still locked in a death grip on the revolver's butt. Marklin would have heard the shots. If he was higher up, closer to Dagger Head, he would have seen it all. Cantrell hoped the man would panic and flee but no doubt his greedy little mind was already calculating the addition of Jovane's share of the silver to his own.

Crouching low, Cantrell began working his way back up the path toward the top of the ridge. He heard no footfalls or horses' hoofs. On the rocks overlooking the precipice a shadow rose up about twenty feet away. Cantrell froze. It was Marklin. But he hadn't seen Cantrell yet. He was craning to look over the edge at the trail far below.

'He's not down there,' Cantrell said, lifting up onto the rocks above the path. He held the rifle's muzzle squarely on Marklin's belly. 'He's back there. Dead.'

Marklin paled suddenly. The rifle in his hands twitched uncertainly.

'Drop it, Marklin. It's over. We know about the silver-mine and why you killed Lieutenant Covington and my wife.'

'Wife? She was a squaw!'

'She'd been taken captive by an Apache raiding party two years ago. I've been tracking her ever since.'

Marklin shifted his weight trying to bring his rifle to bear but Cantrell warned him off with a shake of his head. The man's eyes darted about nervously. His mouth was suddenly filled with cotton. Desperately he wanted a drink of water.

'You raped her,' Cantrell said.

'No! It wasn't me! Beckert did that. I tried to stop him!'

Cantrell's smile was cold. 'You did it. You held Beckert's strings, just like that man down there held yours.'

Marklin felt compelled to shift his gaze, to try to see Jovane's body. He was terrified that Jovane was dead, yet relieved, too.

With a sudden jerk, Marklin pivoted and fired. The bullet caught Cantrell in the fleshy part of the left arm. His body jerked convulsively as he fired. Marklin was working the lever of his rifle when the rocks he was standing on gave way. Hysterically, Marklin screamed. As he fell he doubled over and clutched at the edge of the cliff, releasing his rifle. In that instant Cantrell fired.

'No!' Marklin screamed again. The rocks shattered. His grip destroyed, Marklin tumbled backward, screeching unintelligibly. The fall carried him in a sweeping arc to slam against the trail below. His body bounced once on impact, then slid off the trail into the misty abyss.

Very slowly Cantrell made his way to the top of the ridge and then over to the trail. He moved mechanically now, his body aching and numb. He found Marklin's and Jovane's horses tied to a tree near the trail mouth and started leading them down toward the mine. He met Susan on the trail. She trembled at the sight of him then, crying, ran to him and wrapped him in her arms. He kissed her deeply and long until she eventually pushed herself away.

'You're hurt.'

He nodded weakly. 'A little.'

'I thought they had killed you.'

'Just about.' He tried to smile but it hurt too much. 'I've

159

got to take care of these horses. They're carrying food and water that we'll need.'

'I'll see to the horses, and then I'll take care of you.'

Cantrell huffed out a laugh, remembering how they had met. 'That's a job you keep having to do.'

She smiled and kissed him. 'That's a job I'll keep doing for as long as you need me.'